Welcome to the Sec

It wasn't easy to bring ~~~~~~~~~~~~~~~~~~~~~~
Valley. An important assignment at the plant kept
my dad in the office for long hours. And my mom
got a new account that would keep her away from
home, even on Christmas Day! In fact, everyone in
Paradise Valley, including Annie and Ray, were acting more like Scrooges than Santas. I knew there was
only one sure way to get the entire town back into
the joy of Christmas. But it was going to take a little
holiday magic from a certain GC-161 kid. Forget
Santa Claus, it's Santa Mack to the rescue! Let me
explain. . . .

I'm Alex Mack. I was just another average kid until
my first day of junior high.

One minute I'm walking home from school—the
next there's a *crash!* A truck from the Paradise Valley
Chemical plant overturns in front of me, and I'm
drenched in some weird chemical.

And since then—well, nothing's been the same. I can
move objects with my mind, shoot electrical charges
through my fingertips, and morph into a liquid
shape . . . which is handy when I get in a tight spot!

My best friend, Ray, thinks it's cool—and my sister
Annie thinks I'm a science project.

They're the only two people who know about my
new powers. I can't let anyone else find out—not
even my parents—because I know the chemical plant
wants to find me and turn me into some experiment.

But you know something? I guess I'm not so average anymore!

The Secret World of Alex Mack™

Alex, You're Glowing!
Bet You Can't!
Bad News Babysitting!
Witch Hunt!
Mistaken Identity!
Cleanup Catastrophe!
Take a Hike!
Go for the Gold!
Poison in Paradise!
Super Edition: Zappy Holidays!

Available from MINSTREL Books

NICKELODEON®

the secret world of

ALEX MACK™

Zappy Holidays!

Diana G. Gallagher

A MINSTREL® BOOK

Published by POCKET BOOKS
New York London Toronto Sydney Tokyo Singapore

This book is a work of fiction. Names, characters, places and incidents are products of the author's imagination or are used fictitiously. Any resemblance to actual events or locales or persons, living or dead, is entirely coincidental.

A MINSTREL PAPERBACK *Original*

A Minstrel Book published by
POCKET BOOKS, a division of Simon & Schuster Inc.
1230 Avenue of the Americas, New York, NY 10020

ISBN: 0-671-00084-5

First Minstrel Books printing December 1996

10 9 8 7 6 5 4 3 2 1

Front cover photo by Thomas F. Queally

Printed in the U.S.A.

To my father, Ralph O. Grubel,
with all my love and gratitude
for his understanding and
support over the years.

With special thanks
to Helen Grubel
for contributing information and advice
to the writing of this book.

Zappy Holidays!

CHAPTER 1

Alex slammed her notebook closed with a satisfied smile. Nicole, who was sitting at Robyn's desk, jumped with a sharp intake of breath when she heard the noise.

Sprawled on her bed, Robyn looked up from her history book and said, "What's wrong, Alex?"

"I've just finished my homework," Alex said. "And I hope nothing's wrong. In fact, I'm sure it's all *right!*" Alex began to gather the pens and books scattered on the floor around her.

"You finished all your assignments?" Robyn asked incredulously. "Even your paper on the American Revolution?"

"Which isn't due until Wednesday?" Nicole raised a curious eyebrow.

"Oh, I finished that yesterday," Alex said with a casual wave of her hand.

Robyn and Nicole exchanged disbelieving glances, then asked in unison, "Why?"

Alex didn't blame her best friends for being surprised. She always got her assignments finished on time, but never so far in advance of the due date. "I got it done early because I've got a ton of stuff to do. There's only eighteen days left until Christmas."

"Don't remind me." Robyn shook her head in dismay. "I haven't even started shopping yet, and the mall is going to be an absolute zoo for the next few weeks."

"Maybe not," Nicole said. "I was at the mall yesterday and it didn't seem busy at all."

"That's because everybody's put off shopping until the last minute, like me." Rolling onto her back, Robyn stared at the ceiling. "I am not looking forward to fighting crowds of stressed-out, pushy shoppers. Especially when I know I won't be able to find anything anyone likes anyway."

"I just hate the commercialism." Nicole shook her head in disgust. " 'Tis the season to be greedy. It ruins Christmas for me every year."

"I'm making all my presents this year," Alex said.

Nicole smiled and gave Alex an approving thumbs-up.

"That's why I had to get my homework out of the way," Alex explained. "I'm running out of time."

"Homework is like housework," Robyn said grimly. "It's never done."

Alex just shrugged and glanced out Robyn's bedroom window. The sky was overcast, and a howling wind rattled the bare tree branches against the glass. The bitter cold weather was unusual for Paradise Valley, even in December.

Her friends' attitudes were almost as gloomy, Alex reflected, but they were just being themselves. Robyn was always anticipating disaster, and Nicole had no tolerance for anyone who took unfair advantage of others. Without meaning to they seemed determined to burst the balloon of holiday cheer that had Alex's own spirits soaring. But Alex was not going to let anything—not the drab, winter landscape nor Robyn and Nicole's bleak forecasts about holiday shopping—dampen her good mood.

"So how much schoolwork do you guys have left to do today?"

"Too much." Sitting up, Robyn dangled her legs over the edge of the bed. "My history paper's only half-finished, and geometry leaves me cold. Once I'm out of school, I'll probably never have to calculate the area of a triangle again, so what's the point?"

"You have to know it to pass geometry," Alex said as she stuffed her things into her backpack. "What about you, Nicole?"

"It's a little hard to get psyched about an essay on how George Washington attacked the Hessian troops in Trenton, New Jersey, on Christmas night. That was pretty low, if you ask me."

"He didn't have much choice," Robyn muttered. "The British were stomping all over us, and a surprise attack was Washington's only chance for an American victory. Besides, those German guys were getting *paid* to fight on England's side."

"Washington's troops were threatening to desert because they *weren't* getting paid," Nicole countered.

"But we did get Christmas trees, don't forget." Alex stood up and stretched, then realized that both girls were staring at her with puzzled expressions. "If the English hadn't hired the Hessians to fight for them, the Germans wouldn't have been here during the American Revolution to celebrate Christmas with their decorated trees," she explained. "The colonists thought they were so cool, they started doing it, too."

Nicole nodded thoughtfully. "They used to put real candles on those trees, and then they *lit* them on Christmas Eve. I bet a lot of houses burned down before we had electricity."

"Houses are still burning down because of faulty Christmas lights and wiring," Robyn said.

Alex changed the subject. "It's Friday. You have all weekend to finish that work. Why don't you both come to the park with me?"

"Now? It's freezing out there." Robyn shivered. "I won't get my shopping done if I catch pneumonia. I'm not used to this crazy weather."

"I can't go either, Alex." Nicole shrugged apologetically. "I've got to stop at the store for my mom on the way home."

"What's going on at the park in weather like this?" Robyn asked.

"Nothing. I just need a few good pinecones for the wreath I'm making. That reminds me, Robyn. Can I borrow your Christmas CDs for a couple of days?"

"No."

"Huh?" Alex blinked.

"They're all in the attic, packed away with the Christmas decorations. My dad hasn't gotten them down yet."

"Oh." Refusing to be discouraged, she asked Nicole hopefully, "Do you have any?"

"A few. I'll bring them over tomorrow."

"Great." Slinging her backpack over her shoulder, Alex moved toward the door. "Guess I'd better get going before it's too dark to see. Later."

After bundling into her winter jacket, mittens, and knit cap in the front hall, Alex noticed Robyn's mother sitting in the dining room. She was sipping coffee and staring at a stack of mail on the table. "Bye, Mrs. Russo," Alex said.

Mrs. Russo continued to sip and stare. Realizing Robyn's mother hadn't heard her, Alex quietly let herself out. She was anxious to get started on her gift projects. Making her presents for her family and friends would stretch the money she had saved so she could give something to everyone on her list.

The cold bite of the brisk winter breeze stung Alex's cheeks and blew back her long blond hair as she headed down the sidewalk. She didn't mind, though. The chill was invigorating and made it seem more like Christmas. In spite of her friends' bummed attitudes about the holidays, Alex's enthusiasm for the season flourished.

Her favorite holiday event was when everyone gathered around the huge town tree in the park on Christmas Eve. Every year, just as the sun went down, a switch was thrown and the grand old fir growing in the central grove became a glorious tower of light. Then everybody sang seasonal songs and drank hot chocolate before going home. Even people who didn't celebrate Christmas showed up to enjoy the spectacle and the company of friends and neighbors. It was Paradise Valley's finest tradition.

Many of the kids in school thought that the tree celebration was kind of hokey, a boring grown-up thing to do. But Alex didn't care. She showed up for it every year.

Ducking her head to protect her face from the wind, Alex smiled as she turned onto Oak Street. Maybe she had finally crossed over from kid to adult. Her mother had asked for her Christmas list over a week ago, and Alex still hadn't gotten around to making one. She felt she already had everything she wanted.

"Ooof!" Alex looked up to see she was nose to nose with a gasping elderly man.

She rebounded off the man, whom she had just run into, and stumbled backward a step. Walking with her chin tucked against her chest, she hadn't seen him coming toward her.

"Gosh, I'm sorry," she said. "I didn't see you. Are you all right?"

Clutching his paper grocery bag to his chest, the old man growled at her. "No, missy. I'm not—"

Alex's eyes widened as the wind grabbed the man's hat and whipped it off his head.

"Dang bust it!" As he snatched at his hat, the groceries slipped out of his grasp.

Surprised, Alex reacted automatically and telekinetically grabbed the bag before it smashed on the sidewalk. Realizing what she had done, she instantly let go of it. The old man's gaze darted from his flying hat back to the bag, just as it hit the cement. Fortunately, with the force of its fall broken, the bag landed with a gentle thud and nothing broke. The old man hesitated, staring at the bag for a second.

Alex heaved a silent sigh of relief when he quickly turned his attention back to his hat. Evidently he hadn't seen the paper bag mysteriously pause in midair. He seemed to be more concerned with his hat, which was rolling across the street and into the path of a speeding car.

"Don't you dare run over my hat!" The old man shook his fist at the car as he stalked into the road.

"Stop!" Alex yelled. "It's just a hat!"

"It's the only one I've got!" the old man yelled back without breaking stride.

A quick glance at the hat, the oncoming car, and the old man's course left no doubt in Alex's mind that he was in danger of being run down. She threw up a force field to stop him, then tele-kinetically yanked the hat out of harm's way just as the car sped by. Rolling the hat toward the old man, Alex disengaged the force field, releas-ing him. She picked up the grocery sack as the old man scooped up his hat, jammed it on his head, and stalked back toward her.

"Blasted wind don't know which-a-way it wants to blow," the old man grumbled as he stepped over the curb. "This-a-way and that-a-way. Never been stopped dead in my tracks by no wind before. No, sir." He paused and frowned at Alex. "What're you grinnin' about missy? Think it's funny to watch an old man almost get himself run over?"

"Uh, no, I—" Alex stammered helplessly. She

had been smiling because the old man thought a strong wind had stopped him, but she couldn't very well explain that to him. "I'm glad you're okay, sir. Here's your groceries. I don't think anything's broken."

The man pulled the bag from her outstretched hands. "No thanks to you. Watch where you're going from now on!"

"Merry Christmas," Alex called after him as he turned away.

She glanced back and saw he was glaring at her. "There's nothing merry about Christmas when you're old and alone and living on a fixed income," he replied.

Alex didn't know what to say. Silently she watched him go, with a genuine sense of sadness. She couldn't think of anything worse than being alone on Christmas. She wished there was something she could do to make the holiday merrier for him.

The idea of sharing her holiday spirit with him dispelled the gloom he had left hanging over her, and Alex perked up again. She didn't know what to do for him, but she did know she couldn't do anything if she didn't know who he was or where to find him. Alex decided she had plenty of time to look for pinecones the next day.

Filled with new purpose, she turned away from the park. She followed the old man at a discreet distance until he turned into an alley at the edge of the town's business district.

Hiding in the late afternoon shadows, Alex watched as he trudged up an outside staircase of a large old house. Converted into apartments, the building was badly in need of repair. Yellowed paint was peeling off the walls, and a loose shutter slammed repeatedly against the wood siding. Plywood patches had been nailed over broken glass panes in several windows, and the railing the old man clung to for support wobbled in his hand. If it broke, he'd fall.

Although her powers had gotten stronger as she had gotten older, Alex wasn't strong enough to telekinetically catch the old man before he hit the ground in the same way she had saved the grocery bag. She held her breath until he safely disappeared through a creaking door on the second floor.

The wind blew harder as darkness descended over the town. Few people were out and about, probably because of the unexpected cold spell. And there weren't any streetlights in the alley. Alex's teeth started to chatter as the cold began to seep through her coat. After her encounter with the cranky old man, she was suddenly anxious to get home to her snug and comfortable house. With the wind at her back, Alex hurried along the sidewalk and warmed herself with thoughts of sitting in front of a roaring fire, making Christmas plans with her family.

The Macks always put up the tree at least two weeks before Christmas. Even Annie mellowed during the holidays and enjoyed the family outing to pick out the perfect pine. Alex hoped they would get a tree the following morning, then spend the afternoon and evening decorating it together. Her mom would make hot cider flavored with cinnamon sticks and sprinkled with nutmeg. As they sipped cider they'd wait, secretly amused, as Mr. Mack finished fiddling and tinkering to get the lights arranged just right on the branches. Then they'd talk and laugh as they hung decorations that reminded them of things that had happened on Christmases past. Her mother had kept every ornament Alex and Annie had ever made. And every one of them went on the tree, even though time had loosened the glue holding cotton beards on colored-paper Santas and tarnished the bits of glitter that stubbornly clung to Styrofoam stars. The Mack

Christmas tree was decorated with fond and funny memories, and every year they collected more.

Alex called out cheerfully as she burst through the front door, "Hi! I'm home!" The house was dark and no one answered when she called. Shedding her winter gear, Alex flicked on the lights as she headed into the kitchen. "Mom? Annie?"

Silence was the only answer.

Convinced she was alone in the house, Alex grabbed a soda out of the refrigerator. Annie was probably at the library. Her dad had been working overtime the past week, and her mom may have stopped to do some Christmas shopping after work. They would all be coming home soon, cold and tired after a hard day. But, Alex decided, they wouldn't have to walk into a dark and dismally quiet house.

Humming a winter song about snow, Alex went into the living room and turned on the stereo. After putting a Christmas song collection on the CD player, she turned up the volume and knelt by the fireplace. As she sang along at the top of her lungs, she began to stuff wadded up newspaper into the grate.

"Alex!" Annie yelled. "Turn that down or off or something."

Startled, Alex looked up to see her sister glaring down at her from the top of the stairs.

"And don't sing. I'm trying to study."

"Sorry, Annie. I didn't know you were home." Alex's words trailed off as Annie did an about-face and vanished back up the stairs. As Alex stood up, the front door opened and her parents walked in. "Hi, Mom, Dad."

"Hi, Alex." Mrs. Mack smiled tightly as she dropped her briefcase on the couch, then walked over to the stereo and turned off the music. "I have a splitting headache." Patting Alex on the shoulder, she sighed wearily and headed for the stairs.

Still standing by the door, Mr. Mack sagged like he carried the weight of the whole world on his shoulders. Alex walked over and took his briefcase out of his hand. "Tough day?"

"You could say that." He slipped out of his overcoat and hung it in the hall closet.

"Well, things will look better after you've had dinner, Dad. I'm making your favorite—spaghetti with green peppers and mushrooms."

"That's nice." Taking his briefcase back, Mr. Mack trudged toward the stairs.

Alex couldn't stand it any longer. "What's wrong, Dad? How come everybody's so down? It's Christmas!"

Mr. Mack looked at her with solemn, worried eyes, and said, "Sorry, Alex, but not in Paradise Valley."

CHAPTER 2

Something was terribly wrong.

Alex sat at the dinner table with her family, nibbling at her salad. She was trying to think of the best way to bring up the questions burning in her mind.

Not in Paradise Valley . . . What had her father meant by that? Nothing could stop Christmas from coming—could it?

Alex studied her family's troubled faces. Hardly a word had passed between them since they had sat down to eat. They were all lost in their own thoughts. Finally, she launched into casual conversation, hoping to get them talking.

"How many hundreds of lights do they put on the town tree in the park, Dad?"

"None," Mr. Mack answered bluntly.

"None?"

"Not this year anyway." Mr. Mack absently twirled spaghetti on his spoon.

Alex stared at him for several seconds. The town Christmas tree was one of many community projects that Danielle Atron sponsored to promote her benevolent public image. As the chief executive officer of the Paradise Valley Chemical plant, she donated company funds annually to buy new lights to replace those that had worn out. The plant also paid the electric bill each year to keep the lights shining between Christmas Eve and New Year's Day.

"I don't understand," Alex said to her father. "What do you mean 'none'? The Christmas tree must have a thousand lights on it."

With a weary sigh, Mr. Mack set his fork aside. "Ms. Atron sent a memo around the plant this morning. PVCP isn't going to pay to light the town tree this year."

"Why not?" Alex asked. She couldn't quite grasp what she was hearing.

"The company has had an unusually bad quarter, Alex." Mr. Mack rubbed his forehead and sighed again. "Profits are way down, and Ms. Atron has to cut all unnecessary costs. The company's investors are even threatening to cut our department's funding if we don't make some definitive progress on GC-161 soon."

The mention of the experimental compound that had given Alex her amazing powers broke through Annie's daze. She looked up sharply and asked, "*Are* you making any progress, Dad?"

Mr. Mack shrugged. "It's hard for me to say when I don't even know what GC-161 is being developed to do."

Alex caught Annie's eye, then quickly lowered her gaze. After more than two years of tracking the effects GC-161 had had on Alex, Annie knew more about the properties and potential applications of the powerful compound than anyone, including their father. But unfortunately they couldn't tell him anything that would help his research.

If Mr. and Mrs. Mack knew Alex was the kid who had been doused with the potent chemical, they'd panic. Fearing some awful side effect, they would either take her to the hospital for a medical checkup or to the scientists at the plant for an evaluation. Either way, Alex's life would be ruined. Danielle Atron wanted to find the GC-161 kid almost as much as she wanted to show a substantial profit margin. It was hard enough being Annie's pet science project. Alex had no intention of becoming one of Danielle Atron's scientific pawns, too.

"Why can't the town pay the electric bill for the tree, Mom?" Alex asked, steering the discussion away from GC-161.

Mrs. Mack sighed. "It's not in the town budget."

"Speaking of budgets . . ." Clearing his throat, Mr. Mack glanced around the table. "There won't be any Christmas bonuses this year, I'm afraid."

Mrs. Mack looked up suddenly. "Oh, George."

"I'm sorry, Barbara." Mr. Mack averted his gaze. "I know how much you count on that money—"

"It's not your fault," Mrs. Mack quickly interjected. "It just doesn't seem fair to you. You've worked so hard."

Mr. Mack nodded. "We'll have to go over the household accounts to see if we can't cut some corners of our own."

Alex knew her parents used the Christmas bonus from Paradise Valley Chemical to pay for gifts and extra entertaining expenses during the holidays. Lately she had been telling herself that Christmas was more than presents and parties. Now she had the perfect opportunity to show she meant it. Her parents had enough to worry about without fretting about disappointing her Christmas morning.

"That's okay, Dad," Alex said honestly. "I've got everything I need or want."

Annie gave her a will-wonders-never-cease look, but there was a sparkle of approval in her eyes.

Mrs. Mack smiled at Alex, then clasped her husband's hand. "We'll be okay. Gregory Houston signed a contract with me today."

"City Councilman Houston?" Annie asked.

"Soon to be State Senator Houston," Mrs. Mack said. "I'm his new public relations manager."

"Way to go, Mom!" Alex grinned, delighted to hear some good news.

"That's great, Barbara." The dark cloud of worry vanished from Mr. Mack's face as he beamed with pride and affection.

"I suppose." Frowning slightly, Mrs. Mack shook her head. "But it's a big job. I'm going to be traveling and putting in some long hours—a lot of long hours."

"We'll manage, Mom. Don't worry about it." Alex glanced at her father. "And don't you worry, either, Dad. I'm sure you'll make some kind of breakthrough at work soon."

His smile faded instantly. "Oh, I'm sure I will—but not before a lot of good people at the plant lose their jobs."

Mrs. Mack's eyes widened. "There's going to be a layoff? When?"

"Any day, if the rumors are true," Mr. Mack said wearily.

"Just before Christmas?" Alex was dumb-founded.

"Only Danielle Atron could do something that mean." Annie shook her head in disgust.

"You're not going to get fired because the GC-161 project isn't going well, are you, Dad?" Alex blurted the question without thinking.

Annie and her mother frowned at Alex, then turned to look at Mr. Mack. They all held their breath, waiting anxiously for an answer.

"Danielle hasn't fired anybody, yet." Mr. Mack stood up, his mouth set in a hard, deter-mined line. "Excuse me. I've got some work to finish before I go into the office tomorrow morning. The spaghetti was delicious, Alex.''

''You're working tomorrow morning? But tomorrow's Saturday.'' Alex leaned forward slightly. ''I was hoping we could all go get a tree.''

''I'm sorry, Alex, but our tree will have to wait. Every hour I spend on the job could make a difference.''

No wonder he's feeling so down, Alex thought as her dad left the table. *He's worried about losing his job!*

That's why having to put off the family Christmas tree seemed totally unimportant to him by comparison. Alex's mind raced. Maybe there was some tiny, insignificant thing Annie could tell him about GC-161 that would help him without putting Alex in danger.

Mrs. Mack pushed her plate away and stood up suddenly, too. ''I've got to get started on Mr. Houston's campaign slogans. I don't have the germ of a decent idea yet.''

''Go ahead, Mom,'' Alex said. ''I'll do the dishes.''

''Thanks, Alex.'' Mrs. Mack walked away muttering to herself, *''Nothing* rhymes with Gregory.''

When her mother was safely out of earshot, Alex turned to Annie. "Do you think Dad'll get fired?"

"I doubt it. He knows too much. Danielle Atron doesn't dare let him go."

"That's not exactly true," Alex said cautiously. "Dad really doesn't know much at all about GC-161. So I've been thinking maybe you could—"

Annie's eyes narrowed as she interrupted with, "No way, Alex."

"But you haven't heard—"

"I know what you're going to say, and the answer is no. We can't say anything about GC-161 to help Dad. Not even if it means he'll lose his job."

"But it doesn't have to be anything big, Annie."

"If Dad makes a sudden leap in logic about GC-161, don't you think Danielle Atron will wonder where he got his inspiration? It's just too risky, so forget it."

Alex pressed. "But didn't you see the look on his face? For him, getting fired would be like you getting an F in physics! He'd be totally destroyed. Especially if a lot of people lost their jobs along with him. There's got to be a hint you can give him that won't give *me* away."

Sitting back, Annie stared at Alex for a long moment. "There's more than Dad's job and your personal safety at stake here, Alex."

"Like what?"

"Like . . ." Annie hesitated, considering her words carefully. "Like the balance of world power."

"You're kidding, right?" Alex laughed, then stopped abruptly. Annie was dead serious, not just grasping at straws in an attempt to keep her quiet. "You're not joking."

"Hardly." Moving closer, Annie lowered her voice. "If anyone finds out that an overdose of this stuff produces abilities like morphing and telekinesis, there's no telling how people in positions of power might decide to use it."

"How would they?" Alex asked, intrigued. Her powers came in handy for all kinds of little things on a daily basis, but being able to "think" something off a shelf that was too high to reach or "zapping" on the lights couldn't change the world.

"Picture an army with your powers, Alex."

Instantly Alex's mind filled with an image of

hundreds of silvery puddles charging across a field. She started to giggle.

"It isn't funny. They'd be invincible. Believe me, the longer GC-161 remains an experimental compound that no one understands, the better." Rising, Annie gripped Alex's shoulder. "Better for the world, and better for you."

Alex sighed as Annie headed back to her books in the room they shared. Maybe her sister was just trying to scare her and maybe not. She'd never thought about the potential uses of GC-161 or how dangerous the compound could be if it got into the wrong hands. *Actually, it's already in the wrong hands*, Alex realized as she carried a stack of dishes into the kitchen. If Danielle Atron knew what GC-161 could do, *she'd* be running the world. And that was a really scary thought!

As she rinsed the dishes, Alex hummed Christmas songs to keep herself from sinking into the contagious gloom that surrounded her. It was hard to stay happy when everyone else was feeling depressed and troubled. She wondered why it was that bad moods rubbed off on other people easier than good ones did.

"Hey, Alex!" Ray called from outside the kitchen door.

Alex smiled and dashed to the door to let him in. Ray was the one person she could always count on to cheer her up when she needed it. Nothing ever got him down.

"Hi, Ray!" Alex laughed as she threw open the door. "Boy, am I glad to see you."

Ray didn't charge into the kitchen and head for the refrigerator as he usually did. He didn't smile or say a word. He just stood in the door-way, his shoulders sagging.

"What's the matter?" Alex asked anxiously. "Are you okay?"

"No. I've never been more miserable in my life."

CHAPTER 3

Alex closed the door as Ray shuffled to the kitchen table and sat down. Propping his chin in his hands, he stared at the wall. He looked as though he had just lost his best friend, but she knew that couldn't be the problem. *She* was his best friend and she wasn't lost.

"So why are you miserable?" Alex asked as she slid into the chair opposite Ray.

"The Dynamos traded Paul Sawyer to Chicago."

Alex blinked. "You're bummed out because a hockey player got traded? Is that all?"

"All?" Ray turned slowly to regard her with brooding brown eyes. "He's the best goalie in the league. Without him, the Dynamos don't have a chance of making the play-offs."

"The Dynamos have never made the play-offs."

"Exactly. And they won't make it this year, either. Not without Sawyer. The team manager must be nuts!"

Alex tried not to smile as Ray groaned and covered his face with his hands. Compared to everyone else she had talked to that day, Ray did *not* have a problem. However, the loss of his favorite hockey team's goalie was obviously very important to him.

But it's not that *important,* Alex thought as Ray raised his head and sighed with despair. She couldn't brainstorm an election campaign for her mother or give her father a helpful hint about GC-161. She couldn't stop Danielle Atron from laying off her employees or clear the mall of pushy shoppers for Robyn or change the commercial emphasis on the Christmas season for Nicole. She wasn't even sure she could make the holidays happier for the lonely old man she had bumped into on the street.

But there *was* something she could do.

Alex telekinetically opened the refrigerator door. She knew just the thing to lift Ray's gloomy mood. To distract him, she asked, "How do you know the new goalie won't be better?"

"No way. He's some rookie from Detroit." Sitting back in the chair, Ray folded his arms and contemplated the ceiling.

While Ray talked, Alex "thought" a leftover piece of chocolate cake out of the refrigerator and eased the plate onto the counter. Then she shifted her focus to a drawer and took out a fork.

"His name is Brad Collins," Ray continued. "He was some kind of hotshot on his college team, but that's tame compared to playing for the pros."

"Uh-huh." Alex carefully removed a glass from a cabinet and set it by the plate. "Thinking" a carton of milk out of the refrigerator, she concentrated extra hard as she telekinetically tipped it and poured the glass half-full.

"Well, somebody must think he's good or he wouldn't have been signed to a team." Closing the refrigerator door, Alex lifted the plate and glass and moved them off the counter toward the table.

"Alex!" Mrs. Mack called, dashing down the stairs.

Alex's eyes widened as her concentration faltered. The glass of milk and chocolate cake wobbled in midair.

Ray noticed her expression and turned around. He jumped up and grabbed the hovering glass and plate a split second before Mrs. Mack entered the kitchen.

"I've got to meet with Mr. Houston early tomorrow, Alex," Mrs. Mack said as she approached the table with a slip of paper in her hand. "Would you mind getting a few things at the store for me?"

"Glad to." Alex took the list from her mother.

Still stunned by the close call, Ray stood in the middle of the kitchen, holding the milk and cake.

"Hi, Ray," Mrs. Mack said as she turned to leave. "How are you tonight?"

"Oh, fine, Mrs. Mack. Just fine." When Mrs. Mack was gone, Ray choked back a laugh.

"Careful, Ray. You're going to spill the milk."

"*I'm* going to spill the milk? It would have crashed to the floor if I hadn't saved it—and you!" Laughing softly, he returned to the table and sat down. "That was too close."

Alex shrugged and smiled mischievously.

Picking up the fork, Ray dug into the chocolate cake. "How'd you know I was starving?"

"You're always starving."

Taking a bite, Ray smiled with satisfaction as he chewed and swallowed.

"Wanna watch a movie?" Alex asked before Ray's thoughts returned to his doomed hockey team.

"Sure." Grabbing the milk and cake, Ray followed Alex into the living room. "Got anything new?"

"Nothing you haven't already seen. How about a Christmas classic?"

"Yuck. I hate Christmas movies," Ray said.

Taken by surprise, Alex studied Ray. His bright smile was replaced by a dark frown. He lapsed into a brooding silence for a moment, then quickly recovered. "They're *so* sappy and they all end the same way. Everybody's problems get solved just because it's Christmas. Let's watch something that's got some action."

As much as Alex needed a holiday boost, she didn't argue. Listening to Ray complain throughout a Christmas movie would totally defeat the purpose of watching one. She selected an old horror film and sat down. At least she had managed to take his mind off the Dynamos.

After Ray left, a couple of hours later, Alex gathered their snack dishes and took them into the kitchen. Annie came in and dropped a stack of books on the table. "What are you doing?" Alex asked as she turned on the dishwasher.

"I need a change of scene to clear my head." She flipped open a notebook, and rubbed her eyes. "Have Mom and Dad been upstairs all night?"

"Mom came down to give me a shopping list hours ago, and I haven't seen Dad since dinner." Alex leaned against the counter and shook her head. "I wish there was something we could do—"

"Alex!" Annie cut her off.

"Don't worry. I'm not going to say anything about you-know-what. I meant to do something that would cheer them up a little."

Annie sighed. "That might be pretty tough. I don't think I've ever seen them so worried."

"Yeah." Alex slipped into pensive thought. "Do you think they'd be upset if you and I got the tree by ourselves?"

"We've always gotten the tree together. It would probably make them feel worse if we did it without them."

Alex nodded, then snapped her fingers. "I've got it! You and I could bake Christmas cookies tomorrow."

"Not me, Alex." Annie went to the sink to get

32

a glass of water. "I've got more important things to do than bake cookies."

"What could be more important than making Mom and Dad feel better during the holidays?"

"My future, that's what. The Industrial Scientific Institute scholarship exam is being held the last Friday of Christmas vacation and I've got to cram. If I win, it'll cover all my expenses at the college of my choice." Annie's brow furrowed with worry as she returned to the table. "And it's even more vital now than it was when I signed up a month ago."

"How come?" Alex asked.

"Because if Dad loses his job, he won't be able to afford my college tuition and books." Picking up a pen, Annie turned her undivided attention to her books.

Alex watched Annie for a long moment, feeling totally helpless and overwhelmed. The security she and her sister had always taken for granted was in danger of being snatched away, and there was nothing they could do about it. Tired and beaten down by the troubles that plagued her family and friends, Alex went to bed.

* * *

Alex was late joining her friends in the cafeteria for lunch on Monday.

"It's about time," Nicole said as Alex scooted onto the end of the bench. "Where have you been?"

"I had to return some library books." Alex grinned, glad to be back among smiling faces. Although her parents and Annie had tried to hide their worry all weekend, an unusually tense and gloomy atmosphere had invaded their happy home. Being back in school was a welcome relief.

"Were they overdue?" Robyn asked.

"Yeah."

"No wonder you're late." Ray popped a chip in his mouth.

"You had to listen to Mrs. Winston's lecture, didn't you?" Robyn said.

Alex nodded. "Yeah, and I didn't want to waste time after school. I got my gift projects started over the weekend, but I'll be working on them right up to the last minute."

"I don't want to talk about Christmas presents," Louis said, and then chomped down on his sandwich.

"Me neither," Nicole said with an exaggerated sigh.

Ray nudged Louis and said, "What's the matter, Louis? Have you been so bad this year you're afraid Santa Claus won't bring you anything but coal?"

"This is no time for jokes, Ray. Gadget sales at my dad's store usually skyrocket during Christmas, but they're way down this year."

"I can't believe anyone actually buys your father's weird contraptions," Robyn said.

"Driscoll Do-Whats make perfect gifts for people who don't know what to get someone," Ray said. "Where else can you get a pair of battery-operated socks?"

"Why would anyone need them?" Nicole asked.

Ray and Robyn looked at each other and shrugged.

Louis eyed Nicole narrowly. "Last year your mom bought one of my father's automatic back scrubbers for your dad."

"Oh, yeah," Nicole said. "He liked it a lot—until it stopped working."

"He must have gotten water inside the battery compartment," Louis countered.

Nicole rolled her eyes. "Probably. He was using it in the shower to scrub his back. I don't

35

think my mom will be buying anything from your dad this year."

"No one else in Paradise Valley is, either." Tearing the end of the paper wrapper off his straw, Louis blew into the tube. The rest of the wrapper shot under the table.

"Sales are down, huh?" Alex telekinetically snatched the wrapper from the ground into her hand, then put it into her empty sandwich bag.

"Worse than down. Dad can't even move the stuff at fifty percent off." Shaking his head, Louis placed his half-eaten sandwich on his plate as if he'd lost his appetite. "I don't think I'll be getting a new stereo system for Christmas, and my boom box is dying function by function. It'll only play CDs now."

"That's more than some people have, Louis." Nicole pushed her tray away and lowered her chin onto her folded arms.

Robyn sighed heavily. "Times are tough all over. My dad just found out he has to replace the roof on his business. It's a huge expense he can't really afford right now."

Nobody said anything. Robyn's father owned the only mortuary and funeral home in town.

Alex scanned the downcast expressions on the faces around her thinking, *If everyone doesn't*

*lighten up, they're going to end up with soggy bread
from crying on their sandwiches.*

"How's the toy drive going, Nicole?" Leaning
forward, Alex waited anxiously as Nicole slowly
straightened up. Dedicated champion of the un-
derdog, Nicole was always enthusiastic about
participating in the school's effort to collect toys
for less fortunate children. It was one way she
could help counter the commercialism she
despised.

"Don't ask," Nicole said. "Generosity in Paradise Valley has totally bottomed out. An awful
lot of kids are going to be disappointed if I can't
get people to donate."

"But Mr. Larkin's going to help out, isn't he?"
Alex asked hopefully. The owner of Main Street
Toys and Hobbies always contributed enough
merchandise so every child in town had a
Merry Christmas.

"Not this year," Nicole replied.

"This is starting to look like the worst Christmas ever," Louis said.

"They're all the same to me," Ray muttered
with a faraway look in his eyes.

Alex was glad when the bell rang.

CHAPTER 4

By Thursday afternoon Alex was valiantly struggling to keep her spirits up. School was officially out for the holidays, and Alex planned on making the most of her free time. There were presents to make and cookies to bake and soon, she hoped, a tree to trim. The weather was still unusually cold, and thick layers of dark clouds blotted out the winter sun. Inside the house was almost as cold and dark as outdoors. In an effort to conserve, Mr. Mack had turned down the heat, and everyone was turning off lights that weren't being used.

Annie had taken over the bedroom, demanding not to be disturbed as soon as she got home from school. *That's fine with me,* Alex thought as she sat on the living room floor between her boom box and cardboard craft box. Since their parents wouldn't be home until seven, she planned to work on her dad's gift. Normally, having time alone with the family stereo was almost impossible. This week it had not been a problem.

Sifting through a stack of Christmas CDs, Alex found a collection that had several happy songs with quick tempos. For as long as she could remember, her father enjoyed listening to Christmas tapes in the car while he drove back and forth to work. And every year he complained about having to listen to the slow songs sandwiched in between the fast-paced one. She was making him a tape with only upbeat songs on it, but it was a very time-consuming process. The holidays would be almost over by the time she gave it to him, on Christmas morning. Alex had noticed he wasn't listening to Christmas music in his car very much this year anyway.

But next year things will be better, Alex assured herself as she put the CD in the boom box. She shook off a sudden rush of sadness. She wished that slow Christmas songs was the only thing her dad had to fret about.

Using the stereo remote, Alex set the cassette in the tape deck on record and pause. A cord plugged into the headphone jack on the boom box branched into a Y and connected to the stereo inputs on the deck. She pushed the play button on the boom box and released the pause to begin taping. That done, she pulled out a roll of masking tape and a small beverage bottle from her craft box.

"Sure doesn't look like much," Alex murmured, turning the bottle over in her hand. She skeptically eyed the bits of torn masking tape she had already pressed onto the top half. She had gotten the idea out of a magazine. After the whole bottle was covered with pieces of overlapping tape, she would "paint" it with brown shoe polish, then wipe off the excess before it dried. The shoe polish left along the tape edges and in the recesses would be darker. According to the picture in the article, the finished effect would look sort of like mosaic-cork. Three plastic poinsettias and a candy cane would go inside the bottle. A red bow tied around the neck would finish it off. She had spent the past three afternoons collecting empty bottles with interesting shapes. She was making one for her mother in addition to the pinecone wreath she had hidden in the garage while the glue set. Her grandmothers would love the decorated bottles, but she wasn't so sure about Robyn and Nicole and Ray. She still didn't have an idea for Annie. Humming softly to the energetic strains of "Sleigh Ride," Alex began tearing small, irregular pieces of tape off the roll and pressing them into place.

When the phone rang an hour later, Alex set aside a second bottle and glanced at the tape deck. "Santa Claus Is Coming to Town" was only half-finished. She let it play and dashed to answer the phone. It was Mrs. Mack.

"Hi, Mom," Alex said breathlessly. "What's up?"

"I have to attend a political function with Mr. Houston that came up on the spur of the moment. You and your father will have to fend for yourselves again tonight."

"We'll be fine, Mom." Alex forced a cheerful tone. It was the second time that week her mother had not made it home for dinner, and Alex knew the hectic pace was starting to wear her down. She didn't want to add to her mom's worries.

"I'll keep trying to get your father on the phone, but if I don't, tell him not to bother calling Mr. Alvarado. He already called me to tell me he and Ray have other plans for Christmas."

"Okay." After assuring her mom that everything else was fine, Alex hung up and shuffled back into the living room. She thought it was strange that Ray and his father weren't planning to have Christmas dinner with her family this year. The Alvarados had joined the Macks every year for as long as Alex could remember. Christmas wouldn't seem the same without them.

The Santa Claus song was over, and Alex walked in on the sad refrain of a country-western Christmas tune she didn't know. After listening to a few lines about lost love and lonely hills, she turned the CD off. As she rewound the tape in the deck, her gaze strayed to the dark corner where the Christmas tree should have been, with its bright colored lights and sparkling decorations.

Suddenly, Alex just had to get out of the house. Smiling faces and some bright lights would do wonders for her sagging spirits.

Taking the tape out of the deck, Alex slipped it back into its plastic case and tossed it into the craft box with the CDs. Then she picked up the bottle that was completely plastered with masking tape. She needed to finish it to see how it looked. However, she still had to get the plastic poinsettias and ribbon. That meant a trip to the mall, and the mall was the one place in town guaranteed to be decked out for Christmas.

Feeling better, Alex stashed the boom box and craft box in the garage, left a note for Annie, and grabbed her winter gear. She charged out the front door and ran to Ray's house next door.

"Alex! Come on in before we both freeze!" A gust of numbing wind blew a stack of papers off a hall table as Ray stepped back to let Alex inside. "What are you doing out there in weather like this?" He had to lean on the door to close it against the wind.

"I've got to go to the mall, and I thought you might want to come."

"Don't think so. Nobody in their right mind would walk to the mall on a day like this."

"Well, then I must be nuts, 'cause I'm going," Alex retorted.

"Your toes'll be frostbitten before you get half-way there."

"It's not *that* cold."

"Feels like the Arctic to me!" Ray grinned and shook his head. "Whatever you have to do at the mall can't be that important."

"Oh, it's very important." Alex put her mittened hand beside her mouth and whispered, "I've got to go see Santa Claus."

"Right." The sparkle in Ray's eyes dulled as he frowned and turned away.

"I was just teasing." Alex sighed, confused by Ray's abrupt shift in mood. *Maybe talking to Santa Claus wouldn't be a bad idea,* she thought helplessly. She didn't know what Ray's problem was, but *somebody* had to do something about the outbreak of Christmas blues in Paradise Valley.

"Well, I have to get some things at the craft store, so—" Alex stopped midsentence as the door flew open behind her. Jumping to the side as Ray's father came in, she said, "Hi, Mr. Alvarado."

"Hello, Alex," Mr. Alvarado mumbled. He hurried into the kitchen without a backward glance. Alex sighed. He was probably worried about losing his job at the plant, too. Maybe that's why Ray was acting so touchy.

"It's getting late, Ray. I gotta go," she said.

Ray stared after his dad for a long moment, then lifted his jacket off the coat rack. "On second thought, I'll go with you." Grinning like his old self, Ray held the door open and waved her past him.

Alex was glad for the company, and they

made good time in spite of the cold. Chilled to the bone, they burst through the automatic doors into the heated mall forty-five minutes later.

"Where is everybody?" Ray frowned as he scanned the main concourse.

"Maybe this strange weather's keeping everyone away." Alex looked into the stores on either side of them. Salesclerks were leaning on counters or aimlessly wandering up and down aisles looking totally bored because they didn't have any customers.

"Lucky for us. I really wasn't looking forward to standing in line for hours," Ray said.

Leading the way, Alex headed down the main aisle toward the arts and craft store. Just like years past, the mall's ceiling rafters had been wrapped with bushy green garlands accented by huge red bows and twinkling white lights. Galloping gold and silver reindeer were suspended from the massive cross beams overhead, and giant wreaths decorated with gold balls and red bows hung on the walls. Symphonic Christmas music drifted softly from hidden speakers overhead.

The mall *looked* like Christmas, but it didn't *feel* like Christmas, Alex realized with dismay. The concourse should have been bustling with frenzied people trying to find just the right gift for everyone on their lists. Instead, the mall was practically deserted and eerily quiet. Alex couldn't believe she actually missed getting elbowed and shoved by shoppers.

Alex had no trouble locating plastic poinsettias in the craft store. A bin in the front was full of them. She carefully picked out twenty-one perfect red flowers and a roll of red satin ribbon from a prominent display on the main aisle. Candy canes were not so easy to find.

After searching the whole store, Alex decided to ask a clerk. She approached a man with a clipboard by a display of carved wooden decorations. "Excuse me. Do you have candy canes?"

The thin, sour-faced man peered down at her over the rim of his glasses. "Have you got eyes?"

"Huh?"

"At the checkout!" The man barked and pointed toward the front of the store. "Right there."

"Thank you," Alex said evenly. Hurt by the clerk's unwarranted rudeness, she eased past him.

"What a jerk," Ray said as Alex placed her purchases on the register counter.

The cashier looked back at the man and

sighed. "Don't let him upset you, kids. If business doesn't pick up, he won't have to order any Christmas stock for next year. He can use everything we didn't sell this year . . . if he still owns the store."

"Is it that bad?" Alex handed the woman a ten dollar bill.

"I've been in the retail business for twenty-five years," the cashier said sadly. "And this is the worst Christmas season I've ever seen. Nobody wants to spend money on stuff they don't need when there's a chance they won't be working next week."

"Yeah," Ray said despondently. "I've heard the rumors."

The woman nodded and handed Alex her change. "Everyone depends on the chemical plant."

Alex hadn't stopped to consider the far-reaching effects of a plant layoff. It wasn't just the people who lost their jobs who would suffer. Every business and store in Paradise Valley would be affected, too, like Driscoll Do-Whats. People without jobs didn't have money to spend. Now she understood why even Mr. Larkin was reluctant to donate toys to the town drive. It wasn't because he had suddenly developed a mean and stingy streak. He couldn't afford it.

As Alex stepped out of the craft store, her gaze was drawn to the white structure in the center of the mall. Surrounded by tall artificial pine trees glittering with white Christmas lights, Santa's Castle rose in snow-covered splendor.

Alex hesitated. *It can't hurt . . .*

Ray was several yards down the aisle before he realized Alex was going in the opposite direction. He jogged to catch up to her. "I thought we got everything you needed, Alex?" he asked.

"There's something I have to do, Ray." Handing him the bag of craft supplies, Alex glanced at the Santa display. Groups of caroling dolls dressed in old-fashioned suits and gowns swayed back and forth by lighted lampposts surrounding the raised platform. Mechanical elves moved presents in and out of a toy bag on Santa's big red sleigh. Not a single child was waiting for Saint Nick, but the jolly old man was sitting patiently on his golden throne. He stifled a yawn, then pulled strands of his white beard out of his mouth. His elf helper slipped into her coat and waved as she left. Santa stood up and stretched.

Ray's eyes widened. "You're not going to— You can't! What if someone sees you, Alex? You'll never live it down."

"I don't care," Alex said stubbornly. "Besides, there's no one here to see me." Turning on her heels, Alex mounted the steps and paused behind Santa as he hung up the SANTA'S FEEDING THE REINDEER sign. "Have you got a minute?" she asked tentatively.

"I've got all the minutes you need, young lady." Santa turned and smiled warmly.

Alex knew the man had just been hired to play Santa Claus, but the face that looked down at her was slightly wrinkled with age, and his beard was real. His cheeks were flushed pink, and his blue eyes twinkled with kindness.

"Is there something special you want for Christmas this year?"

Alex nodded. "Yes. I just want everyone in Paradise Valley to be happy again."

Santa chuckled and said, "That's a pretty big order in this town right now."

"Yeah. My dad's working really hard to save everyone's jobs at the plant, but he can use all the help he can get. I, uh, just thought I'd let you know."

"I'll see what I can do, but—" Sighing, Santa pulled a small candy cane out of his pocket and gave it to her. "Is there anything else? Something you want for yourself?"

"Nope. That's it." Smiling, Alex hurried away.

"Take care, Alex!"

Alex stopped dead and whirled around. *How does he know my name?* She couldn't ask because Santa was disappearing through an employee door between stores. Baffled, Alex stared at the Santa sleigh. A mechanized elf, who was supposed to be shaking a strap covered with bells, wasn't moving.

Ray stepped up beside her. "So what did you ask for?"

"For everything to be all right in Paradise Valley again." With a quick look around, Alex zapped the mechanism inside the elf. The little figure jerked as the bolt of electricity from Alex's fingers shot through his mechanical inner workings. Then he began blinking his eyes and jingling his bells again.

Ray watched the elf with a somber expression and sighed heavily. "Some things can't be fixed that easily, Alex."

"What do you mean?" Alex started, shaken by a deep and unexpected sadness in Ray's eyes. It vanished almost instantly, as though Ray were used to suppressing some unknown, but very deep pain. But it was too late. She had seen it.

Ray shrugged. "Nobody can fix a whole town, Alex. Not even Santa Claus."

CHAPTER 5

Feeling worse instead of better after her experience at the mall, Alex arrived home to find that things had not improved there, either. As she paused by the entry hall to hang up her things, Mrs. Mack charged in. Alex quickly tossed the shopping bag with the ribbon, flowers, and candy canes into a corner of the closet so her mom wouldn't see it.

"Hi, Mom. I thought you were going to be late tonight."

"I'm not staying. Excuse me." Mrs. Mack reached in front of Alex to pull her good winter coat off a hanger. "Do I look all right?"

Alex cocked her head. Her mom was wearing

a tailored dark suit over a white blouse with a large, distinctive collar. A gold chain and small gold earrings added just the right touch of elegance to the outfit. "You look terrific," Alex said sincerely.

"At least something's going right today." Slipping into her coat, Mrs. Mack began shifting things from her everyday purse to a small, chic black one.

Alex could tell her mother was frazzled and desperately in need of some relaxation after her grueling first week as Mr. Houston's public relations manager. "Tomorrow's Friday, Mom. We can get our Christmas tree after you and Dad are off work and—"

"I can't think about Christmas trees now, Alex," Mrs. Mack snapped. "I'm late." She stormed out the door, slamming it behind her.

Alex stared at the closed door, stung by her mother's abrupt dismissal. *Why is she mad at me?* It was more than Alex could take. The lingering shreds of her Christmas spirit disintegrated, leaving her as completely depressed as everyone else. She went into the living room and paused to stare out the window. The night was as dark as her mood. Clouds hid the moon and stars, and the chilling wind howled through the branches of leafless trees.

Her father walked in from the kitchen. "Did your mother leave?"

"Yeah." Alex sighed. "I think she's mad at me, but I don't know why."

"She's not mad at you, Alex." Mr. Mack came up beside her and stood with his hands in his pockets. "She's upset because she's not going to be home for Christmas."

"What?" Alex was sure she hadn't heard him right.

"Mr. Houston wants to attend a big benefit dinner the governor's holding in the capital on Christmas Eve, and your Mom has to be there. It'll be the official launch of his campaign on a state level." Shifting uncomfortably, her father stared at the floor. "She was on the phone all afternoon, but she can't get a plane back until the day after Christmas."

"Then she can't go!" Alex simply couldn't imagine spending Christmas without her mother.

"She has to go, Alex. Your mother can't risk losing the Houston account in case I lose my job. And if I don't come through with something guaranteed to improve the plant's financial prospects next quarter, I *will* lose my job." With slumped shoulders, Mr. Mack walked away.

More miserable than she had thought possible, Alex flopped on the couch. Her father was right after all. Christmas wasn't coming to Paradise Valley.

This year nobody was interested.

Exhausted, Alex didn't want to do anything, go anywhere, or see anyone. Zapping on the TV, she stretched out and yawned. The commercial ended and the Vintage Movie Channel resumed, showing a classic black-and-white version of *A Christmas Carol*. As she watched the ghost of Christmas past take Scrooge back to the loneliness of his school days, she was reminded of what Ray had said.

Nobody can fix a whole town. Not even Santa Claus.

Or Charles Dickens's three ghosts, either, Alex thought. They only had to fix the attitude of one Scrooge, and he was rich.

When the movie was over, Alex went up to bed. She drifted into a restless sleep and had nightmares about Christmas trees.

She walked onto a Christmas tree lot and the needles fell off every tree she touched . . . then every tree she looked at. The grotesque image of a hundred pine tree skeletons faded, and she found herself staring up at an artificial tree near Santa's Castle in the mall. It was leaning slightly, and she telekinetically reached out with her thoughts to straighten it. The little bell-jingling elf she had zapped yelled, "Timber!" as the tree fell to the floor with a deafening crash. A thousand lights crackled and popped and went out . . . and she was suddenly back in her own living room. A decorated Christmas tree stood in the corner. She plugged in the lights to turn them on and nothing happened. She zapped the string. The beautiful tree caught fire and turned black in the blaze. . . .

When she woke the next morning she remembered the dream. The details all came back to her, but in the light of day it didn't seem so real. She sat up and stretched, recalling the movie she had watched before she went to sleep, about that old meany Scrooge.

And then she remembered that it was the first day of Christmas vacation! Alex jumped out of bed, determined to make the best of it. Everyone around her—her friends, her family, the whole town—could look on the grim side if they wanted to. But that didn't mean she had to. People had the freedom to change their minds and look on the bright side if they chose to. *Maybe that change should start with me*, Alex told herself. Even Scrooge had changed his ways, with some persuasion.

Could she persuade the whole town?

Annie entered the room and frantically began shuffling through the papers on her desk. "It's got to be here . . ." she mumbled.

"Lose something?" Alex asked.

"My pass into the exam!" Annie stood back and ran her hand through her tangled hair. "It's in this mess somewhere."

Alex looked at the clutter on Annie's side of their room. Books and notebooks were scattered on her bed and around the floor. Her older sister was usually perfectly organized. But exhaustion and stress were having an adverse effect on her habits. In addition, she simply didn't have enough space for so much study material.

"You'll find it," Alex said. She smoothed out the sheets and blanket, then began tucking them in.

"What are you doing?" Annie asked with a perplexed frown.

"Making my bed." Alex pulled the bedspread over her pillow.

"You just got up."

"Uh-huh." Most days Alex was so rushed or

busy she never got around to fixing her bed. It drove Annie to distraction, and Annie didn't need any additional distractions before her exam. Alex wasn't at all sure how to activate the Christmas spirit in a whole town. She just figured that if bad moods could rub off on other people, then good ones could, too. So home—and more specifically, her bed—seemed like the best place to start.

"There." Alex gave her pillow a final pat, then began collecting her dirty clothes. She felt Annie watching her as she dumped the clothes into the laundry basket in the closet. After grabbing clean jeans and a sweater from a drawer, she paused by the door. "If you need to use my bed to sort your stuff, feel free."

"Uh—okay. Thanks." Annie looked at Alex as if she didn't quite trust her sister's generosity.

Grinning, Alex ducked into the bathroom.

After a quick shower, Alex dressed and ran downstairs, singing "Deck the Halls." Her father was in the kitchen, gulping a last cup of coffee before he left for the plant. Alex stopped in the doorway and bellowed, "Fa-la-la-la-la . . . la-la-la-LAH!" Then she executed a sweeping bow.

Mr. Mack smiled. "You're certainly in a good mood this morning."

"It's Christmas!"

Setting down his cup, her father looked past her into the living room. "It sure doesn't look like Christmas, though, does it?"

"No, but it is anyway. We don't need a tree and presents and stuff to have a merry Christmas, Dad. Just being together is all that's important, right?"

Mr. Mack stared at her thoughtfully a moment. "That's exactly right." He almost smiled again, then sighed instead. "Except we won't . . ."

Mr. Mack left without finishing his sentence, but Alex knew what he was thinking. They wouldn't be together because her mom was going to be stuck out of town with no way home. That problem was beyond her power to solve, so she put the unpleasant thought out of her mind. Thinking about it would only make her sad, and she had to stay happy no matter what. Besides, strange and wondrous things happened at Christmas. Maybe Mr. Houston would change his plans.

For the present, she had to concentrate on her own plan. *The house doesn't look like Christmas,* Alex thought as she began pulling the baking utensils out of the cabinets. *But it's sure gonna smell like Christmas in a little while!*

She was taking her first sheet of Christmas cookies out of the oven when her mother finally came down for coffee.

"Smells wonderful!" Mrs. Mack peered over Alex's shoulder and sniffed. She nodded with approval as Alex scooped hot cookie stars and bells off the tin and put them on a cooling rack. "They look great, too."

"I just hope they taste as good as they look." Alex slid a second sheet of cookies into the oven and set the timer.

Mrs. Mack poured herself a cup of coffee and leaned on the counter. "I wish we could bake together as usual, but I've got a ton of paperwork to catch up on today."

"That's okay, Mom." Sprinkling flour on the counter, Alex began rolling out another pile of dough. "Are you gonna work here or at the office?"

"I'll probably get more done at the office."

"How'd the dinner go last night? Is Mr. Houston happy with your PR program so far?" Alex asked. Picking up a large Santa cookie cutter, she pressed it into the dough.

"So far so good." Mrs. Mack took a sip of

coffee, then sighed heavily. "Your dad said you were very upset because I won't be home for Christmas. I don't want to go to the benefit, Alex. You understand I don't have a choice."

"I know. We'll work it out. Somehow we're going to be together for Christmas."

"Please, don't get your hopes up, Alex. Every plane and train is booked solid with long standby lists." Mrs. Mack turned away to wipe a tear from the corner of her eye.

Alex pretended not to notice. After putting silver candy balls on the Santa cookies, she pushed the tray aside. Then she picked up one of the baked star-shaped cookies and held it out. "Have a cookie and make a wish, Mom. Who knows? Maybe a Christmas wish will come true."

Mrs. Mack hesitated, then took the cookie and shrugged. "Why not? You could be right."

Alex smiled. "I believe in Santa Claus."

"Yeah. Me, too." Mrs. Mack took a bite. "Very tasty."

"Really?"

"Really." Giving Alex a quick kiss on the cheek, Mrs. Mack started for the stairs, then stopped. "Funny, but you know what?"

"What?"

"I know this doesn't make sense, but I've got the strangest feeling I *am* going to get home for Christmas." Laughing softly, Mrs. Mack headed up the stairs.

This just might work, Alex thought hopefully as she began rolling more dough. In a couple of hours she had scored one and a half smiles from her dad, and her mother was even laughing.

"Did you find your exam pass?" Alex asked when Annie entered the kitchen weighed down by a backpack stuffed with books.

"Yeah, thanks." Dropping the bag by the door, Annie wandered over to the counter and said, "I think Mom's losing it."

"Why do you say that?"

"She's in the bathtub singing about being home for Christmas." Annie reached for a cookie, took a bite, and gave Alex a thumbs-up. "I can't believe she's not going to be here. I think Mr. Houston is a total jerk to make her miss Christmas."

"She's not going to miss it."

Annie sighed. "Listen, Alex. I wish it could be different, too, but I'm not going to delude myself about the realities of the situation. She has to go to the campaign dinner, and there's no way back by Christmas morning."

Alex calmly continued cutting stars. "We'll see."

"You've got an acute case of wishful thinking," Annie said.

"*Positive* thinking, Annie. It's not the same thing."

Grabbing a couple more cookies, Annie hoisted her bag and left for the library.

Alex picked up a star cookie, closed her eyes, and took a bite. "Mmm," she said. Then she looked at the door Annie had just closed and said, "I don't care what anyone says. I'm positive my wish will come true."

CHAPTER 6

Securing the plastic wrap over a paper plate full of cookies, Alex stepped outside the front door. She hesitated in pleasant surprise. The wind had died down and the sun was peeking through the clouds. She smiled as she started up the sidewalk toward town, almost believing her high spirits were having a positive effect on the weather, too.

She still hadn't thought of a way to make the entire population of Paradise Valley forget their troubles, but she wasn't going to let that deter her. She was just going to take it one person at a time until inspiration struck—starting with the lonely old man she'd bumped into. Alex had made dozens of cookies that morning and hoped he would accept some of them as a peace offering.

As Alex turned into the alley leading to the old, rundown apartment house, she heard a plaintive *meow* overhead. Looking up, she saw a small orange tabby cat clinging to a high, over-hanging branch in a nearby tree. Setting the plate on the ground, Alex held up her hand and tried to coax the cat down.

"Come on, kitty. It's all right. . . ."

The cat lifted one paw, then thought better of it and dug into the bark with its claws.

Alex glanced around the alley. Assured that no one was watching, she focused her powers on the cat. The animal resisted the telekinetic tug at first, but as Alex gently raised it off the branch, it finally had no choice but to release its grip. However, it did not quietly surrender to the frightening force that was lowering it toward the ground. The cat's piercing, terrified yowl shattered the afternoon stillness.

"Percy?" a shrill voice called out. A plump old woman came scurrying around the corner of a neighboring house as the cat's feet touched the ground. "What are you doing to my cat?"

Pausing just long enough to hiss at Alex, the

cat took off and leaped into the old woman's arms.

"Nothing. It was stuck up in that tree—"

"A likely story. You should know better than to pick on helpless animals."

"I wasn't picking on him. Honest," Alex pleaded. "I like cats."

"Maybe." Cradling Percy, the woman scowled uncertainly. "What business have you got hanging around here anyway?"

"I'm delivering these cookies to the man who lives up there." Alex pointed to the second floor of the next house.

"Hah! And just why would you or anyone else want to bring cookies to a cranky old coot like Trucker Thompson?"

Alex smiled. "So he won't be cranky anymore."

"That'll be the day." Shaking her head, the old woman hurried toward her house, on the corner.

Alex noticed that it wasn't in much better shape than Mr. Thompson's building. Another elderly lady, thinner than the first one, met the woman at the door. She set down her knitting needles and yarn and took the cat.

"Merry Christmas!" Alex hollered and waved.

The two women looked at her, looked at each other, shrugged, then closed the door.

Sighing, Alex mounted the rickety stairs to Mr. Thompson's door. She remembered not to lean on the unstable railing. The rusty nails securing it to the steps were all pulling loose. On the landing, she saw that one of the boards was rotting through. Being careful not to step on it, she pushed the doorbell but didn't hear a chime sound inside. She banged a tarnished, brass door knocker and waited. After a moment footsteps thumped on a wood floor and the door flew open.

"What'd ya want!" The old man glared at her and jutted out a chin covered with the graying stubble of a beard. His thinning silver hair was uncombed, and his rumpled sweatshirt was spotted with food stains.

"Uh, well, actually—" Alex stammered nervously, then forced a smile. "I thought you might want some Christmas cookies, Mr. Thompson. I made them myself." Alex held the paper plate out to him. "I'm sorry about running into you last week."

The old man's eyes narrowed. "How'd you know my name? You been spying on me?"

Alex shook her head. "No. The lady who lives down there told me."

The old man glanced toward the corner house. "Which one of those miserable old crones has been talking about me?" He didn't give Alex a chance to answer. "Doesn't matter. Both of them think they've got a right to mind everybody's business."

Alex just shrugged, then flinched as Mr. Thompson turned his angry gaze on her again.

"And if *you* think a few cookies will make up for almost getting me killed, missy, you can just forget it," he growled. "They probably taste awful anyway."

Alex jumped as the door slammed in her face. Disheartened, she started to leave. She took a few shaky steps down the stairs, then turned back. Mr. Thompson was the crankiest old man she had ever met. *A real challenge,* she thought. If she could spark a little Christmas goodwill in him, she could spark it in anyone.

Leaving the cookies on the landing, Alex ran down the stairs. Concentrating on the brass knocker, she telekinetically pounded it against the door, then ducked under the stairway. Just as she slipped out of sight, she heard the door bang open.

"Go away and leave me—"

Even though she couldn't see him, Alex could picture the old man's perplexed expression. It wasn't as if she were playing a mean prank on him. She wanted him to have the cookies and a merry Christmas, too, if that was possible. She didn't have a clue what to do about that, but she was confident she'd think of something.

"Well," Mr. Thompson mumbled, "don't know how she did that, but the little scamp sure don't give up easily." Then he laughed softly.

Alex pressed her mouth tightly closed to keep herself from laughing out loud. She could add another chuckle to her score. If it wasn't for Annie's pessimism, she'd be batting a thousand.

After the door slammed shut, Alex stepped out of hiding and looked up. The plate of cookies was gone. Heading back out the alley, she saw two faces pressed against a window in the corner house. A curtain suddenly fell closed, and Alex grinned. The two elderly ladies were minding her business, too, but that was okay. They were too far away to have seen the door knocker bang by itself. And maybe she had added a little zest to an otherwise dull day by making Mr. Thompson laugh.

Next stop—Nicole.

*   *   *

When Mrs. Wilson showed Alex into the family room, she found Nicole and Robyn sitting on the floor, staring at a blank TV screen. "What are you doing?" Alex asked.

"Nothing." Robyn sighed.

"I can see that. How come? I thought you'd be running around town collecting toys."

Nicole shrugged. "We were."

"Hi, guys!" Ray sauntered in with a smile on his face and a pillowcase slung over his shoulder.

Reinforcements, Alex thought. Two smiling faces were better than one. *And if I can make it four . . .*

"Why are you walking around with a pillowcase, Ray?" Robyn asked bluntly.

"Alex wasn't home, so I figured she was helping you round up toys. Thought I'd lend a hand, and I had to have some way to haul the loot."

"There is no loot," Nicole said despondently. "Ms. Clark said that if we don't make any progress in the next couple of days, the drive will be canceled."

"Canceled?" Alex didn't understand why the teacher advisor for the toy drive would want to give up. "That doesn't sound like Ms. Clark."

Nicole shrugged. "It's not her fault. It has

something to do with the school board and government regulations. We either have to have enough toys for everyone or we can't give them to anyone. Guess it'll be none, 'cause nobody wants to donate anything."

"Only broken or worn-out stuff has been donated." Robyn pointed to cardboard boxes by the sofa. "We quit because we didn't want to cart home a lot of junk we'd just have to throw away."

Alex glanced into a box. A teddy bear with a missing nose and no plush left on its cloth body was draped forlornly over the edge. She picked it up and was struck by how sad it looked.

"This could be fixed," Alex said. "With a new nose and some clothes, he'd look kinda cute."

Nicole took the bear and studied it with a critical frown. "I suppose, but I'm not exactly handy with a needle and thread."

"Neither am I," Robyn said.

Alex lifted a wooden toddler's puzzle from the box. It was a picture of a clown. The pieces were all there, but the paint was scratched. "And this just needs some new, nontoxic paint."

Raymond peered over her shoulder and pulled two toy cars from the box. "We could use the parts from one of these to fix the other."

Sudden understanding dawned on Nicole's face. She smiled and jumped up with energized enthusiasm. "A lot of people were willing to give us broken toys. If they're all fixed up to look like new and work like new, the kids wouldn't care, would they? I mean, getting a new-looking used toy would be better than no toy at all, right?"

"Right," Alex said.

"Good thinking, Alex." Ray patted her shoulder.

"Except for one little detail you haven't considered," Robyn said.

Leave it to Robyn to find the downside, Alex thought. However, if the idea was flawed, they were better off knowing about it now. "What little detail?" she asked.

"Even if the four of us could make doll clothes and repair cars—and I'm not sure we're *that* talented—we don't have the supplies, the tools, or the time. Nicole figures we need over a hundred good toys and Christmas is only ten days away."

Ray slumped. "I hate to admit it, Alex, but sh's got a point. We'd still have to go out and collect more used toys, too."

"I'm sure we can get some other kids to help with that." Alex was not about to give up. It was a good idea, and she was determined to make it work . . . somehow.

Nicole tossed the bear back into the box and said, "Collecting isn't the problem. I can find volunteers, but I can't sew to save myself."

"I flunked finger-painting." Robyn made a face. "All my pictures came out brown."

"That's because you mixed all the colors together," Ray explained.

Robyn threw up her hands. "And all these years I never knew!"

Nicole began to pace in agitation. "So how do we turn junk into toys worthy of Santa Claus?"

"Too bad we don't have an in with Santa's elves," Ray quipped.

"That's it!" Alex's eyes widened as an idea burst full-bloom into her mind.

Nicole peered at Alex quizzically and said, "Don't tell me you've got an in with Santa's elves."

"Maybe I do." Alex nodded and smiled mysteriously. "Maybe I do."

CHAPTER 7

Alex led her friends down the sidewalk. Each of them was carrying a box of broken toys. All the while Nicole, Robyn, and Ray badgered her with questions about who the mysterious elves could be. She hadn't answered their questions because she wasn't actually sure the elves she had in mind would accept the job.

But I won't know until I ask, Alex thought as she turned into the alley. *Nothing ventured, nothing gained. . . .*

"Your elves don't live in a very cool part of town," Ray observed with an anxious glance over his shoulder. Long shadows fell across a drive lined with overflowing trash cans.

Robyn shivered and said, "This is certainly not how I pictured the North Pole."

"Trust me." Alex started singing "Jingle Bells" to distract them, and Nicole, Robyn, and Ray joined in. Not only did the song relieve their apprehension, it attracted attention. Alex smiled as the two old women in the corner house rushed to the window to investigate the racket. She hoped they wouldn't be able to resist coming out to see what was going on.

"Wait here." Leaving her bewildered friends a short distance from the old man's house, Alex mounted the stairs with a cardboard box tucked under her arm. As she expected, Mr. Thompson threw open his door and snapped at her.

"Don't you have anything better to do than pester me? What do you want now?"

"Help," Alex blurted out. "I need your help, Mr. Thompson." She held her breath, waiting for the old man to slam the door in her face again. But he didn't. A subtle shift changed his expression from annoyed anger to guarded curiosity. He stole a glance into the box, then peered at the kids below.

"Who's that?" he asked.

"My friends. Nicole is running the junior high

Christmas toy drive and we're helping her. I'm Alex Mack.'' She held out her hand.

Mr. Thompson ignored it. "I don't have any toys!"

"I know." From the corner of her eye, Alex saw the two elderly women bustling toward her friends. "There are lots of kids in Paradise Valley who won't have any new toys for Christmas, either—unless we do something about it."

"We?" Folding his arms, Mr. Thompson raised an eyebrow. "And just what do you think *we* can do about it? *If* we wanted to—which we don't."

Alex explained in a rush, realizing that Mr. Thompson was interested regardless of his words to the contrary. Otherwise, he would have gone back inside. "All we can get is broken stuff people were going to throw away," Alex finished. "But most of it can be easily fixed."

Mr. Thompson scowled as he peered into the box. He picked up a pull-toy train with a broken string. "You're probably right about that—Hey!"

Alex looked down below her as Mr. Thompson shook his fist over her head. Nicole was talking and gesturing as the old women poked through the toys in the cardboard boxes on the ground.

"Get out of there, Mabel Porter!" Mr. Thompson shouted.

"This is a public alley, Trucker!" the plump woman huffed. "Irene and I have *business* here!"

Trying not to grin, Alex followed as Mr. Thompson stomped down the stairs. She wondered if Trucker was his real name or a nickname. Noting the furious flash in his eyes as he charged across the drive toward the old women, she decided that this was not a good time to ask.

Planting himself in front of Ms. Porter, Mr. Thompson waved the toy train in her face. Ray, Nicole, and Robyn watched the confrontation with perplexed fascination.

"Alex came to me with this project—not you!" Thompson exclaimed.

The elderly man was much taller than the thin lady, Irene Porter, but she was not intimidated. "For your information Nicole is in charge of the toy drive and she just asked *us!*"

"What do you know about making doll clothes, anyway?" Mabel Porter asked him.

"And I suppose *you* can repair battery-operated gizmos!" Mr. Thompson countered.

"Hold it!" Raymond whistled and moved in between the arguing elders. "Time!"

Everyone shut up.

"This job is too big for one person." Ray looked at the old man, then at the two women. "Or even two. I'm not even sure the three of you working together round-the-clock till Christmas Eve can get it done."

"There's a hundred kids out there who believe—beyond a doubt—that Santa Claus won't let them down," Nicole said.

"If we don't have enough toys," Robyn added, "we'll have a bunch of unhappy kids."

"It'll take cooperation and teamwork to pull this thing off," Ray finished.

Mr. Thompson's frown faded as he scanned the solemn young faces before him. Rubbing his bristled chin, he looked at the two women. "Truce?"

The Porter sisters exchanged glances and nodded. "Truce."

Alex sagged with relief.

"That's the elf spirit!" Ray said, grinning broadly.

"Elf? Since when do elves come in six-foot sizes?" Mr. Thompson asked indignantly.

"Since now," the plump woman answered.

Mr. Thompson laughed. "If the shoe fits—"

The Porters hustled everyone into their kitchen and out of the cold. Over mugs of hot chocolate, they dubbed themselves the elf squad and made their plans. The corner house would be the head-quarters and workshop because it was bigger than Mr. Thompson's apartment. And as Ray pointed out, they wouldn't have to tote boxes of broken toys and supplies up and down the stairs. Starting Monday, the collection division would begin an intensive door-to-door cam-paign. None of the kids' teachers had assigned homework over the vacation, so they could work from morning to night. Nicole was sure she could find more kids to help. They needed to collect hundreds of broken toys in order to have enough fixable ones, plus parts.

Flushed with a warm inner glow, Alex listened to the discussion. Being united in a common cause had dissolved the animosity among the se-nior members and had routed the kids' blues. Mr. Thompson playfully flirted with the elderly sisters, and they giggled with girlish pleasure. Nicole, Ray, and Robyn talked with increasing excitement, determined to make sure that every child in Paradise Valley had something from Santa under the tree on Christmas morning. Six more depressed, frowning faces had been trans-formed into smiling ones. *Only a few thousand left to go*, Alex thought as she and the other kids waved good-bye.

Nicole and Robyn headed home to begin their phone campaign to sign up collection volunteers. Alex and Ray tackled the stores in town, hoping to convince the owners to donate supplies. They didn't pressure anyone. They just explained the purpose and needs of the project, then left the Porters' phone number. Most of their contacts were too preoccupied and worried to show much interest. However, there was one bright moment. The manager of the Center Street Hardware Store thought he had some nontoxic, craft-quality paint sets with brushes in his storeroom. They had not sold when he had them on the shelves. He told them to come back Monday.

In spite of her success with friends, family, and the elderly elves, Alex's spirits took a downward plunge as she and Ray walked home. Despair had the entire town by the throat, and she couldn't think of any way to loosen its grip. The task was just too huge for one teenaged girl, even one with amazing powers. Ray's earlier good humor and positive outlook had waned, too, she noticed as they took a shortcut across the park.

''Don't worry, Ray. We'll get the toys done.

I'm sure of it." Alex tried to sound confident, hoping to lighten her own mood as much as his.

"It's not that." Sighing, Ray kicked a stone.

"Then what?" Alex had known something was bothering Ray for over a week. Whatever the problem, he was hiding it well. Most of the time he kept the sadness buried, and she had been too busy to press him.

"Nothing." Ray walked a little faster.

Alex paced him. "Come on, Ray. This is me, Alex, your best friend. What's wrong?"

"I don't want to talk about it, okay?" Ray snapped. Then he stopped and took a deep breath. "Sorry. Guess I'm just tired or something."

"Yeah. Me, too." Alex knew Ray was holding something in, but her instincts told her it was not the right time to pry. He would confide in her when he was ready. "It's getting colder, too," she said to cover the awkward moment.

"Wind's coming up again." Ray pulled his jacket collar up to protect his ears.

Nodding, Alex looked out over the wide expanse of parkland. Her gaze came to rest on the towering fir tree that was used as the town Christmas tree every year. Its dark silhouette against the evening sky was a too-perfect symbol of the desperation that hung over Paradise Valley. A lump caught in Alex's throat. If the tall tree was ablaze with thousands of sparkling Christmas lights, the sight would make her feel better instead of worse—

Alex's heart fluttered.

The tree!

"Yes!" Alex raised her fists to the sky and laughed.

Ray eyed her skeptically and asked, "Did I miss something?"

Alex shook her head. She didn't want to discuss her sudden flash of inspiration. Although she had figured out what to do, she didn't know how to do it. Lighting the town tree wouldn't be easy, but she had to believe with all her heart and soul that she *could* do it. In his present mood, Ray might try to talk her out of trying.

But she had to do more than try. She had to *succeed.*

CHAPTER 8

Ray and Louis were knocking on Alex's door at nine o'clock sharp Monday morning. Nicole called at 9:01. Alex offered the boys doughnuts, then wandered into the living room with the cordless phone. To keep her spirits up, she turned her back to the corner where the family Christmas tree should have been.

"Ray and Louis just got here, Nicole," Alex said into the phone. "They'll meet you at the Porters' house in a few minutes."

"You're not coming?" Nicole sounded frantic. "We only found ten other kids who said they'd definitely show up to collect old toys."

"Our elves can't fix broken toys if they don't

have supplies," Alex said practically. "I'll go get the paints from the hardware store and then I'll stop by the other stores in town. Then I'll make a list of anyone who has something to donate and we can send a team out to pick up the stuff later." Alex had given her plan of action a lot of thought while she was working on her masking tape bottles the day before. She needed time alone to pursue her own campaign to light the park tree, but she didn't want to let Nicole down, either.

"Okay." Nicole exhaled with relief. "Thanks, Alex. Tell Ray and Louis we'll be waiting for them. I've worked out a grid of the different neighborhoods, but even working in teams of two it'll still take all week to cover the whole town."

"We'll get the job done. Stop worrying." Alex hung up and grabbed her coat from the hall closet. She sympathized with Nicole. Christmas was a week from tomorrow, and there was so much to do. Alex hadn't planned on devoting so much time to the toy drive when she had first decided to make gifts. She had finished the pinecone wreath and the poinsettia arrangements for her mother, grandmothers, Robyn, and Nicole, but she still didn't know what to do for Annie or Ray.

Her parents had worked at home the day before, so she hadn't had a chance to work on her father's Christmas music tape. And she was still determined to see the town tree lit up, too.

"At least the weather's on our side," Louis said as he left the house with Alex and Ray.

Alex nodded. The sun was shining and the temperature had risen to a tolerable forty-five degrees. The warmer weather would make roaming around town more comfortable, but she had been secretly hoping the unusual cold and cloudy weather conditions would bring snow. It rarely snowed in Paradise Valley, and she had never had a white Christmas.

Louis whipped out two Santa Claus hats and handed one to Ray. "A little bit of psychological prodding," he explained.

"Yeah." Ray put on his hat and grinned. "Who could refuse to give something to such charming Santa's helpers?"

Alex was glad that Ray's dark mood had passed. He was genuinely enthusiastic about the toy drive, but she knew that his unknown problem hadn't gone away. He had just buried it again. She intended to ask him about it when the time was right.

Parting company with the boys at the corner,

Alex promised to check in at Elf Headquarters at lunchtime with her supply donation list. When they were out of sight, she turned in the opposite direction and headed for the Paradise Valley Power and Light Company, on the edge of town.

The receptionist in the lobby tried to hide her amused surprise when Alex asked to see the plant manager. Undaunted, Alex assured the woman that her business was important and wouldn't take long. Five minutes later, the receptionist ushered her into Mr. O'Leary's office.

"Have a seat, Miss Mack," the manager said.

"Thank you." Alex sat and launched into the pitch she had been practicing in her head. Mr. O'Leary listened attentively, but his expression was grim when she finished.

"I wish I could help you, but there isn't enough time."

"Why not? Don't you just have to throw a switch or something?"

"The tree is usually plugged into a circuit that's powered off a second meter in the park storage shed. We install and activate the meter every December and bill Ms. Atron. However, she's canceled the service this year."

"Yes, I know, but—" Alex sensed that Mr.

O'Leary wanted to help. "Can't the power company donate the electricity?"

"We could, but this is a government regulated utility. By the time I process all the paperwork to get approval, Christmas will be long over."

"Oh." Alex frowned. "Just out of curiosity, how much does it cost to light the tree during Christmas week?"

"Well, let's see. I can't access Ms. Atron's records because they're confidential, but maybe I can give you a rough estimate." Mr. O'Leary turned to his computer and mumbled as he worked. "They use those big outdoor lights . . . so that's ten thousand lights at twenty-five watts per bulb—"

"Ten thousand?" Alex gasped.

"Approximately. That tree's over sixty feet tall." Mr. O'Leary continued his computations. ". . . five cents per kilowatt hour and the tree's usually lit from five P.M. till one A.M. That's eight hours a day for nine days . . ." He tapped the keyboard, hesitated, then looked back at Alex. "Seventy-two hours comes to just under nine hundred dollars."

"Nine *hundred* dollars?" Alex's mouth fell open.

"Twelve dollars and fifty cents per hour . . .

plus tax." Mr. O'Leary shrugged. "I guess that look on your face means you don't have enough money saved to foot the bill."

"I couldn't even pay for an *hour*."

Mr. O'Leary nodded. "Have you talked to City Hall?"

Alex shook her head. "Lighting the tree isn't in the town budget."

"No, but maybe someone could authorize the expense out of petty cash," Mr. O'Leary suggested.

"Like Mr. Houston, the city councilman?"

"Yes. I really would like to help, but—"

"Well, thanks for taking the time to listen anyway." Rising, Alex started to leave, then handed the manager one of the cards she had made up with the Elf Headquarters phone number. "If you have any old toys you'd like to donate to the toy drive, call this number and we'll send someone to pick them up."

"*Old* toys?"

Alex quickly explained the problem with the toy drive and her solution. Mr. O'Leary promised to have his wife find something useful to contribute.

Confident that Mr. Houston would see her, Alex hurried to his law offices, across the street from City Hall. Alex knew that authorizing the lighting of the town tree would be great publicity for a man trying to get elected to the state legislature. However, unlike the power company's friendly receptionist, the thin man in Mr. Houston's front office was cold and inflexible.

"I'm sorry, miss, but Mr. Houston's schedule is full and you do *not* have an appointment."

"But it's very important to the town."

"Everybody's business is important to the town. Mr. Houston is not in at the moment anyway." Scowling, the man checked a book on the desk. "I can fit you in on January eighth . . ."

"Never mind." Alex considered telling him that she was related to Mr. Houston's public relations manager, then decided against it. For one thing, she didn't think he would be impressed enough to make an exception. In addition, using her mother's name and position to pressure her way through the councilman's door might have unpleasant repercussions. What if her mother lost the account because her daughter had rudely intruded on Mr. Houston's limited and valuable time?

Unwilling to give up, Alex left and marched across the street to City Hall. If she found Mr. Houston there, she would approach him as an ordinary citizen with a vital issue to discuss. If not, there were other people on the city council and a mayor.

None of the town officials in City Hall were available to listen to a nonvoting teenager's problem.

On the verge of defeat, Alex trudged away from the mayor's office. Halfway down the hall, she passed an open door and casually scanned the lettering stenciled on the glass. She stopped and backed up to read it again: ELLEN GRABLE, CITY FINANCIAL OFFICER.

Might as well give it a shot, Alex thought. She walked into the outer office, but no one was sitting at the desk.

"Hello?" Alex called out tentatively.

A small, gray-haired woman with a kind smile appeared in a doorway off to the side. She was wearing a green and red Christmas sweater with big white snowflakes. "Can I help you?"

"I hope so. I'd like to speak to the financial officer."

"That's me. Come on in." Standing aside, Mrs. Grable motioned Alex into the office. "What can I do for you?"

Perched on the edge of a leather armchair,

Alex once again outlined the reasons why the town tree should be lit regardless of the cost.

"I agree with you completely, Miss Mack, but I can't authorize that expenditure. The town can't afford it."

"It's only for a week." Alex didn't understand. Nine hundred dollars was a fortune to a junior high student, but not to a city.

"A day or week, it doesn't matter. A significant portion of Paradise Valley's operating money comes from the municipal sales tax. The city's revenues are down because retail sales are down. We can't spend more than we take in. It's a state law."

"I didn't know that." Alex's head spun. Even the city government was being affected by the bad financial situation at the chemical plant. Because people faced losing their jobs, they weren't buying things. And because they weren't buying things, the town's income from taxes had been reduced. She hadn't realized economics was so complicated.

Mrs. Grable sighed. "You see, we have to cut spending somewhere. You wouldn't want a policeman or a firefighter to take a cut in pay because the town wasted funds lighting up a tree, would you?"

"No, I wouldn't."

"Of course not. The city payroll has to take priority over unnecessary expenses—such as Christmas trees."

"What about petty cash?'" Alex asked hopefully.

"Unfortunately, the money in that account can only be spent for specific purposes outlined in the town charter, and Christmas decorations are not included. We can't use money designated for one thing to pay for another. That's the law, too."

"So there's no way." Out of options, Alex exhaled wearily.

Mrs. Grable leaned across her desk. "There's no way the *town* can pay for it. Maybe you could take up a collection—"

"No. Everybody's so worried about being unemployed, they can't even donate toys for the kids who need them. Nobody's gonna give money to light up a tree."

"I see." Mrs. Grable sat back. "And I'm sorry to hear about the toy drive. So many parents on limited incomes depend on it every year."

"That project's not nearly as hopeless as the tree." Seeing the flicker of interest on Mrs. Grable's face, Alex explained and handed the woman her hand-printed card. "If you don't have any old toys, we can use all kinds of sewing and craft supplies."

"I've been saving leftover bits of this and that for a long time. Boxes and boxes of it are just gathering dust in my garage. Maybe the elf squad can put it to good use." Mrs. Grable smiled thoughtfully. "In fact . . . could you use another elf?"

"We can use every elf we can get. Thanks."

Alex gave Mrs. Grable the Porters' address, then began going from store to store in search of more supplies. She was encouraged by the interest everyone showed in the modified toy project. Easily half the people she talked to had something unwanted, but potentially useful, to donate.

But no one wanted to discuss a Christmas tree that cost twelve dollars and fifty cents per hour—plus tax—to light.

CHAPTER 9

Clutching a cardboard box full of craft paints from the hardware store, Alex stood in the doorway of the Porter sisters' house and stared. The elderly women's quiet, sedate home was in chaos.

Plump Mabel Porter and three older women Alex had never seen had a cookie-baking production line going in the kitchen. The counters were littered with bowls, spoons, measuring cups, rolling pins, and cookie cutters. The tantalizing aroma of baking cookies, chocolate, nutmeg, and cinnamon filled the air.

Wiping her hands on her apron, Mabel Porter shooed Percy the cat away from her feet, then moved a sheet of waxed paper covered with flattened dough to the woman on her right. "I think we need more Santas, Ruth."

"Santas or bells, Bessie?" Ruth called to another woman taking two tins of baked cookies out of the oven.

"Both!" Bessie called back.

The woman on Mabel's left handed her a ball of dough she had just finished mixing. "Thanks, Angie," Mabel said. "Let's go for another batch of chocolate chip. Ruth's arthritis might start bothering her if we don't give her a break from cookie cutting."

Angie saluted smartly. "Gotcha."

Another woman walked in with an empty plate and said, "The cookies passed the taste test."

Mabel scowled at the crumbs on the plate. "At the rate those old coots are testing them, there won't be any left for the kids."

Alex took a hesitant step inside and almost collided with Mr. Thompson as he rushed past her with a jar of dirty turpentine and paint brushes. "Oops. Sorry, Mr. Thompson." She blinked and looked again at the old man. He had shaved and combed his hair and appeared quite handsome.

Mr. Thompson eyed her sternly. "You're just bound and determined to knock me off my feet, aren't you?" Then he winked and smiled. "How's the search for supplies going?"

"Fine. I've got more paint and a list of places with donations. I've covered most of the stores in town. This afternoon I'll go to the mall."

"Wonderful. The paint goes in the dining room, and the list goes to Nicole. She's coordinating all the teams." Mr. Thompson nodded toward the living room.

"Who *are* all these people? What's going on?"

"Well, it seems Paradise Valley is just full of senior citizens who always wanted to be Christmas elves. Cool, huh?" Grinning broadly, Mr. Thompson continued on across the kitchen. "Excuse me, Bessie. I gotta use the sink for a minute."

"Take your time, Trucker." Smiling pleasantly, Bessie began drying the dishes draining in a plastic rack.

Alex edged her way through several men and women working on wooden and plastic toys in the dining room. The worn carpet was covered with sawdust, and the table was covered with newspapers, jars of turpentine, paint, and brushes. Robyn walked around the end of the table, making notations on a clipboard.

"Okay. That's eleven plastic cars, four metal trucks, three wooden pull toys . . ." Spotting Alex, Robyn waved.

"Where should I put this box?" Alex called over the loud buzz of an electric jigsaw set up in a corner.

A short, stout, balding man turned with a smile. Splatters of blue paint freckled his rosy cheeks. He was holding a doll with one re-painted eye. "Good question, young lady. We're a little short of room."

"Put it under the table for now," a woman across from him suggested.

As Alex put the box down, Ray came up behind her with a pillowcase full of stuff slung over his shoulder. "Whoa!" he said. "Looks like Santa's workshop needs to expand already."

Louis followed, bent over with the weight of a cardboard carton heaped with old toys. "Find me a spot! Quick! I can't hold onto this much longer!"

"Under the table, Louis," Robyn said.

Louis dropped the box and rubbed his aching arms.

"Yes, ma'am!" Unslinging his pillowcase, Ray

pushed it under the table with his foot. "What are the chances of two starving field elves getting some of those cookies?"

"Ask Ms. Mabel. She's in charge of the kitchen," Robyn said. Then she motioned for Alex to follow her.

"Who donated the supplies for all those cookies?" Alex asked.

"The elf squad. Senior citizens get monthly coupons for free basic foodstuffs like flour and sugar. They all pitched in their coupons."

The living room had become the sewing center and Nicole's command post. Irene sat in a rocker, sewing an arm back onto a stuffed dog. Other ladies were knitting and sewing clothes for an assortment of stuffed critters and dolls piled around them. Ms. Clark, the school advisor, was on the phone in the corner.

Nicole sat cross-legged on the floor by the coffee table. Papers and maps were strewn on the sofa behind her. "Hey, Alex! I was beginning to wonder where you were."

As Alex pulled the supply donation list out of her pocket, Mrs. Grable from the city financial offices came in through the front door with a carton.

A wiry, little man with glasses took the box from the woman.

Mrs. Grable looked over and recognized Alex. "Hi there!" she said with a wave.

"Hello, Mrs. Grable."

"I've got to get back to work now, but I'll see you all later!" Mrs. Grable scurried back out the door.

The man with Mrs. Grable's box looked around the cluttered room helplessly. "We just don't have enough space, Nicole."

"Yeah. I know." Brushing stray wisps of hair off her face, Nicole scanned Alex's list. "This is great, but as you can see, we don't have anywhere to put more stuff. And we're getting more volunteers and boxes every hour."

"A couple of other people have offered to let us use their apartments, but nobody wants to split up the group," Robyn said.

Looking at the content and happy faces of the industrious elderly elves, Alex understood. The energy and camaraderie generated by working together would be lost if the elf squad was broken up into smaller units. "There must be some place in town that's big enough to hold everyone."

"I'm open to suggestions," Nicole said.

"I've got one. . . ." Robyn stared at the floor and chewed her lip for a moment before looking up.

"We're listening." Mr. Thompson handed Robyn an updated list of collected toys that were fixable.

Robyn clipped the paper to her clipboard. "My dad said he wanted to help out. His business is on a large estate—"

"We can't move the elf squad there!" Nicole gasped.

"Why not?" Mr. Thompson asked.

"Robyn's father owns Russo's Funeral Home." Alex held her breath as everyone in the room stopped what they were doing to stare at her.

"We may be old, Alex, but we're not dead, yet." Mr. Thompson sighed and rubbed his chin. "But Nicole is right. That's not the proper location for Santa's Workshop."

"Actually," Robyn said, "moving into the main building is not what my dad had in mind. There's a large heated garage with a huge second-floor apartment that has kitchen facilities on the property. It's a good distance away from the business, but close to the main road with a separate driveway. It's also surrounded by trees, completely out of sight of the funeral home."

"Sounds perfect," Mr. Thompson said.

"And the sooner we start moving everything, the easier it's gonna be," Irene said with an emphatic nod.

"Okay. I'll call my dad right now." Robyn returned a few minutes later to say that her father would be delighted to have the elves set up shop in his garage.

Leaving the squad to handle the move, Alex hurried on to the mall. The momentum and support the toy drive was gaining as word spread from one person to another was encouraging. Alex was heartened to see that Paradise Valley wasn't totally lacking in seasonal spirit. However, she soon realized that the elf workshop was only a small oasis of cheerful goodwill in a vast desert of despair and gloom.

A number of shoppers strolled up and down the mall concourses, but they weren't struggling to carry bags overflowing with gift purchases as one would expect during the holiday. Many were leaving shops empty-handed even though several windows displayed banners announcing drastic price reductions. After visiting half the stores, Alex finally had to admit she was wasting her time. Unlike the independent owners of the businesses in town, the managers of the large chain stores could not give away anything without permission from their corporate headquarters. The store managers, too, were in danger of losing their jobs because of low sales.

Anxious to get back to the joyous company of the elves and her friends, Alex headed toward the exit. As she passed Santa's Castle, she couldn't help overhearing two young mothers talking while they waited for their children to finish visiting the jolly old man.

"I know my husband's right. We can't afford to buy toys for Alice this year, not if he's going to get laid off at the plant." The woman sighed deeply. "But she's only five! What's she going to think when Santa doesn't bring her anything?"

"I know," the other woman said sadly. "I know."

Alex edged closer. A small blond girl sat on Santa's lap, and an older boy was waiting his turn nearby. She glanced at their worried mothers, suddenly realizing that they didn't know about the toy giveaway every Christmas morning. Apparently they had always been able to buy toys for their children. However, she wasn't sure if they'd be willing to accept any kind of charity.

The little girl's face glowed with excited anticipation as she jumped off the platform into her mother's arms. "Santa's gonna bring me a doll with extra clothes," she cried out.

"He will if he can, honey."

Alex glanced at the piece of paper she had brought along to list stores willing to make donations. It was blank. *But not for long*, she decided as she stepped over to the child and smiled. She would put it to another use.

"Excuse me. I'm Santa's secretary elf."

"What's that?" the child asked.

"It's my job to write down your name and what you want, so Santa doesn't forget." Alex saw the girl's mother frown uncertainly. "But first I have to ask your mom something, okay?"

"Okay." The little girl ran to the far side of the platform to watch the caroling dolls.

Alex chose her words carefully as she explained that the senior citizens of Paradise Valley had gotten together to repair old toys for Santa to hand out Christmas morning. She went on to say that the project had filled their lives with purpose.

"They'll be awfully disappointed if no one shows up at Santa's Workshop to collect," Alex said.

"I see. Well, I wouldn't want to be responsible

for making Santa's elves unhappy." The girl's mother gave Alex her daughter's name and said, "She wants a doll with extra clothes."

After jotting down the little boy's information, Alex asked them to pass the word on to others. The elves would do their best to see that every child got what he or she wanted.

After the women left, with bright smiles on their faces, Alex turned to see Santa watching her curiously. No other children were waiting in line, so she mounted the steps and walked over.

"Hi, Alex." Santa winked. "Seems to me you're doing a pretty good job of making some folks happy without my help."

"A few people, maybe, but actually, I do need your help." Alex smiled sheepishly. "How do you know my name?"

"I'm Santa Claus."

Alex didn't press him. She confessed to volunteering his services as the elf squad's official Santa Claus Christmas morning. "Your, uh— boss won't get mad if you help us, will he?"

"I don't have a boss. Business is so bad at the mall this year, the management can't afford to pay me. I'm doing this for free because the children need a Santa Claus to talk to."

"Will it be too much trouble to keep a list of toys the kids want?"

"Trouble? Until this moment I've been the loneliest, unhappiest Santa in mall history. Now, just like that, I've got elves and a workshop and bunches of toys to deliver on Christmas morning. It's no trouble at all; it's my job."

Alex grinned as he laughed aloud. His belly shook and his eyes really did twinkle. And she suspected that under his white beard he had merry dimples, too.

"And as the official Santa Claus, I really must know what you want for Christmas, Alex."

Shaking her head, Alex started to leave, then hesitated. She looked back at Santa and said softly, "My mother."

Santa frowned. "Something's happened to your mother?"

"Not exactly. She's Councilman Houston's public relations manager, and she has to be in the state capital Christmas Eve. She can't get transportation back until the twenty-sixth. Even the car rental places are overbooked." Alex couldn't stop her eyes from misting over. "I just want her home for Christmas, but—"

Santa nodded solemnly. "I'll find a way, Alex."

"I wish I could believe that, but I know that even you can't do the impossible."

"Nothing's impossible," Santa said earnestly. "You've proven that. A week ago, who would have believed that dozens of lonely senior citizens would be having the time of their lives setting up shop as Christmas elves? And because of them, a lot of children will have a merry Christmas, too. You made it happen because you believed in yourself and you didn't give up."

"I suppose—"

"Believe in me, too, Alex."

Something in the man's intense gaze filled Alex with hope. She didn't know who the man was or what he did the rest of the year, but he certainly had the heart of the real Santa Claus. And if Santa couldn't get her mother home in time for Christmas, no one could.

CHAPTER 10

The week passed quickly, and Alex was gratified by the response the toy project received.

Volunteers of all ages contributed supplies, broken toys, time, and talent to the elf squad. Local restaurants took turns supplying lunch for the workshop crews, and stores placed posters with the time and address of Santa's giveaway in their windows. Mr. Hardwick, editor of the *Paradise Valley Press*, wrote and published an article about the elves and agreed to print a large announcement without charge the weekend before Christmas. Santa Claus himself came by every day to deliver his lists and a happy ho-ho-ho of encouragement.

In spite of his own financial problems, Robyn's father went out of his way to help, too. He posted a big SANTA'S WORKSHOP sign at the end of the driveway and set up a computer in the shop. Then he took charge of coordinating the repaired toys with Santa's lists from the mall. Assigned toys were tagged with the child's name, and he tracked down requested toys the collection teams hadn't been able to locate.

Although the circle of Christmas cheer continuously expanded, Alex was sadly aware that most of the town's population could not escape the threat of a bleak and uncertain future. No one knew from one day to the next if they'd still have a job the following morning.

Alex left the workshop early Friday to visit her father at the plant. Danielle Atron was not throwing the usual lavish holiday party for her employees and their families. However, she had invited everyone to stop by to collect a small token gift that afternoon. Mr. Mack had asked Alex to make an appearance so the CEO wouldn't be offended. Annie was too busy cramming for the scholarship exam. Alex had agreed, but only for her father's sake.

As she approached the front doors of Paradise Valley Chemical, Alex felt a slight twinge of apprehension. It wasn't likely that Danielle had set another trap to catch the GC-161 kid, but caution was always advisable. Alex's fears proved to be unfounded. The lobby of the administration building was deserted except for Dave, one of the plant's drivers. Dressed as a Christmas elf complete with pointed green shoes and a Santa hat, he was asleep in a chair by the door. A bag of candy canes dangled from his hand. Tiptoeing past him, Alex ducked down a hall and went directly to her dad's office.

"Hey, Alex!" Mr. Mack looked up from his computer and grinned. "I was beginning to wonder if you were going to make it. There hasn't been a very large crowd so far. I think Ms. Atron's upset."

"It's her own fault, Dad. She's the one threatening to fire people."

"There will be no layoff, Alex." Mr. Mack rubbed his neck and stretched. "Not if the results of these lab tests proves what I think they will."

Alex tensed. Had the lab tests revealed something significant about GC-161? That could be good for her dad, but bad for her. "You mean you've discovered something about—"

Mr. Mack put a finger to his mouth.

"—you-know-what?" Alex finished.

"Not a thing. I've been working on something else."

"What?" Alex asked, genuinely curious.

"I call it Ac-Not. Apply according to the directions on Friday, and a pimple's completely gone by Sunday."

Alex understood the implications instantly. Teenagers plagued by acne would try anything to cure the problem, even if the treatment didn't help. A medication that actually worked was worth a fortune. No wonder her father had been toiling day and night to complete the development phase.

"If this compound is as effective as the preliminary tests indicate and we get FDA approval, Danielle will have to keep everyone working to manufacture it. And that means the company will soon be making a huge profit."

"That's great, Dad! I'm so proud of you." Alex threw her arms around his neck and hugged him. "We should celebrate. You and I could get the Christmas tree on our way home."

Mr. Mack shook his head. "I wish I could, Alex, but I can't. Dan Wilcox is an excellent lab technician, but I've got to supervise the testing process to make absolutely certain nothing goes wrong. Too much is at stake for too many people."

Alex forced a smile and murmured, "I understand, Dad."

Mr. Mack pulled out his wallet and said, "But you've waited long enough for your tree."

Hiding her disappointment, Alex took the twenty dollar bill he held out. Buying the tree by herself wouldn't be the same as sharing the event with her family. But maybe her mother and Annie would be home later, ready to take a break from the pressures of work and study to help decorate it. Either way, just having the Christmas tree up and shining in the vacant corner might improve everyone's spirits.

"Oh, and by the way—" Mr. Mack stopped Alex as she turned to leave. "I'm really proud of you, too, Alex. Everyone's impressed with the wonderful job you and your friends are doing with the toy drive. The elf squad is the talk of the town."

Flustered and pleased by her father's praise, Alex felt her cheeks begin to tingle. Her father had a hard time expressing his feelings, and Alex was always taken by surprise when he did. Bidding him a quick good-bye, she turned and left before he noticed the golden glow—one of the more troublesome results of her encounter with GC-161.

On her way out of the building, Alex couldn't avoid Dave.

"It's not much," Dave said as he handed her several candy canes, "but it's better than nothing."

Pocketing the candy canes, Alex hurried down the lighted drive toward town and the Christmas tree lot. As she passed the park, she was drawn to the dark towering tree in the center. Standing under the canopy of its lower branches, she saw that the city hadn't bothered to string the thousands of lights. Without money to pay for the electricity to turn them on, there was no point.

Saddened by the sight of the forsaken tree, Alex shuffled away. Sometimes there was nothing anyone could do. . . .

A sudden gust of wind whipped around her, rustling the massive branches of the tree. Alex paused and looked back. She stared at the tree, but her thoughts focused on her father's determined efforts to develop a money-making product so no one would be fired. Racing the clock and against all odds, he had worked relentlessly to accomplish the difficult task of saving the chemical company and its employees. Now he was only a few lab results away from success.

Her father hadn't given up.

The branches of the mighty tree whispered in the wind.

Alex listened. Win or lose, she couldn't give up, either.

CHAPTER 11

It was almost seven o'clock when Alex pulled the Christmas tree through the front door. Walking into the dark, quiet hall, her hopes of finding her mother and sister home were instantly dashed. She flicked on the lights and leaned against the doorway for a moment to catch her breath. Then she dragged the tree into the corner of the living room and propped it against the wall. An intense sorrow began to seep into her thoughts, but she fought it off. Coming home to a decorated house would lift her family's spirits, so Alex set about the task with a determination that matched her father's.

Singing along to the songs playing on the

boom box, Alex brought several boxes of decorations in from the garage. She had actually managed to finish her father's cassette tape and decided to check it for flaws. In addition, just in case her father wanted to hear a particular selection, she was listing the songs with the digital count so they'd be easy to find. So far the tape was perfect and the happy songs energized her.

After the boxes were lined up on the couch, Alex lugged in the heavy Christmas tree stand her grandfather had made when Annie was still a baby. He had mounted a red and green metal stand on a bushel basket filled with flat rocks. She smiled as she telekinetically positioned the tree trunk in the metal holder and tightened the large screws. She could almost hear her grandfather say, "Nothing short of a tornado can topple a tree in that contraption." As she stood back to make sure the tree was standing straight, Alex realized he was right. No Mack tree had ever toppled, not even the year her father had tripped over a roller skate and fallen into it. A few broken ornaments had been the only casualties.

"Winter Wonderland" ended and Alex jotted down the counter numbers for "Frosty the Snowman."

Another fond memory surfaced when Alex

opened the first box and found a wad of silver tinsel icicles lying on top. When Annie was eight she wanted to get the tree a week early. Alex and her mother had thought it was a great idea, but their father was set on waiting. He gave in when he found Annie putting tinsel on the large, plastic rubber plant that had once stood in the same corner. Alex concentrated on the music as she searched for the lights. Remembering past Christmases wasn't nearly as much fun alone.

Ray rang the doorbell as Alex was untangling strings of lights and checking them for burned-out bulbs.

"Am I glad to see you, Ray! There's nothing worse than decorating a Christmas tree by yourself. Well, almost nothing."

"You're decorating your tree?" Ray hesitated on the threshold, then shrugged as he walked in. "Guess that's still better than being at home."

"What's wrong at home?" Alex asked, puzzled.

"Nothing." Ray glanced at the boxes on the couch, shook his head, and sat on the floor. He was not smiling and he was definitely annoyed.

Now is *the right time,* Alex thought as she sat down opposite Ray and continued testing the lights. She had to approach the subject of his dark mood carefully or he'd just refuse to talk about it again. A few awkward minutes passed with only the sound of Christmas music pouring from the boom box speakers.

"I'm depressed tonight, too," Alex said finally. Maybe sharing the way she felt about her mother missing Christmas would prompt him to discuss his problem.

She was about to say more, but Ray suddenly jumped and hit the buttons on the boom box.

The music stopped.

Ray propped his chin on his knees and traced a lazy pattern on the carpet with his finger. Alex waited, too stunned to say anything. In all the years she and Ray had been best friends, she had never seen him so upset and—angry. *At me?* She wondered, but she didn't think so.

"I'm sorry, Alex," Ray said after a couple of long, anxious minutes. "But I just can't listen to that stuff right now." He took a deep breath to calm himself. "What were you saying?"

"My, uh . . . mother's tried everything she can think of, but . . . there's just no way she can get back from the capital in time for Christmas."

"At least she's coming home, Alex."

Alex stared at him. *How could I have been so dense?* Ray's mother was never coming home.

She had died of a sudden and unexpected illness several years ago. He never mentioned her, but that didn't mean he didn't miss her—especially at Christmas.

"Ray—I'm sorry. I wasn't thinking. I—"

"It's okay, Alex." Ray sighed heavily. "It's not your fault my dad is being such a jerk—again."

Thoroughly confused, Alex frowned. "Your dad?" She couldn't imagine anything that could disrupt the warm and loving bond Ray shared with his father.

"Yeah. I mean, I understand that he misses my mother. I do, too. And I suppose that losing her is one of the reasons we're so close—except at Christmas. All the hurt comes flooding back, and he totally withdraws from everything and everyone, including me. Right now, as far as he's concerned, I don't even exist."

"I'm sure that's not true, Ray. Your dad loves you—"

"Not enough to care how I feel."

"How come you never told me?"

Ray shrugged. "I guess I didn't want you feeling sorry for me. Besides, there was no reason to ruin your holidays just because mine were miserable."

As Alex thought back to past Christmases, she

realized that she should have noticed something was odd. When he was younger, Ray never went to visit Santa Claus or talked about what he wanted. And she realized that Mr. Alvarado had always seemed distant and withdrawn during Christmas dinner. Ray had been covering up the problem for years.

"Have you told him how you feel, Ray?" Alex asked.

"No."

"You've got to tell him."

"No."

Deep in her heart, Alex knew that Ray's father wouldn't deliberately hurt him. Somehow, she had to make Ray see that. "That's not fair, Ray. No one can solve a problem unless they know there *is* a problem."

"No!" Ray's eyes flashed. "I don't want him pretending to feel something he doesn't out of guilt! He wants to drop out and feel sorry for himself during Christmas. He just doesn't care what happens to me."

Alex was sure Ray was wrong, but she also sensed that he was too hurt and confused to understand right now.

A button on the boom box suddenly snapped up.

"That's funny." Ray picked up the box and stared into the cassette window. "Oh. The tape just ended. I must have turned down the volume instead of turning it off."

"Rewind it for me will you?" Alex asked. She checked her notes and realized she hadn't written down the count for the last few songs. "Frosty" was the last song with a number. "Back to nineteen-hundred-ten on the counter. I'll listen to the rest of it later. Want some popcorn?"

"When have I ever turned down popcorn?" Ray grinned.

"Never. It was a silly question."

A few minutes later, Alex handed him a bowl of buttery popcorn.

"I stopped your tape on seventeen-eighty," Ray said.

"Close enough." Alex popped an action movie starring a comical pair of cops into the VCR, then paused before pushing the play button. "Can I ask you something?"

"Sure." Ray tilted his head back and dropped popcorn into his mouth.

"Well, it's just that you seem to be having such a good time helping out at the toy workshop and all. I was just wondering why, since Christmas stuff bothers you so much." Alex tensed slightly as Ray paused to consider his answer. She didn't want to upset him, but she needed to know.

"It's fun. And I like all the elves. They're old, but they're cool, too. I mean, Mr. Thompson acts so tough, but he's really a nice guy. Working with them takes my mind off how things are at home. When I come over here, I'm just reminded of how things *should* be at my house." Ray shrugged apologetically.

"Yeah." Things were not as they should be at her house, either, but Alex didn't say so. Compared to Ray's situation, her family had been having a great time the past couple of weeks.

"It's hard to explain," Ray went on, "but doing something to make all those kids happy makes me feel better."

"Maybe something like that would make your dad feel better, too," Alex said tentatively. "Helping someone, I mean."

"Forget it. No way he'll become an elf. He can't even stand to hear Christmas carols this time of year."

"That's not exactly what I had in mind. He's pretty good with tools and stuff, isn't he?"

Ray nodded.

"Well, maybe he'd help you fix Mr. Thompson's wobbly railing and the squeaking hinge on the Porters' back door . . . if you asked. There's also a rotting board on Mr. Thompson's landing and a loose shutter. They've done so much for us and the kids. It would be a nice Christmas present for them."

"I'll think about it." Picking up the remote, Ray turned on the movie.

End of discussion, Alex thought as she sprawled on the floor. Checking the lights brought her thoughts back to the big town tree. Knowing that the fun-filled atmosphere at the workshop made Ray feel better reinforced her belief that lighting the tree in the park would have the same effect on the unhappy residents of Paradise Valley. She still had ten dollars set aside to buy something special for Annie, but ten dollars would buy forty-six minutes of electricity.

Forty-six minutes isn't much time, Alex thought as she stood up and searched through the boxes for the star that went on the top of the tree.

Dave's apologetic words, when he'd given her the candy canes, darted through her mind. *Not much, but better than nothing. . . .*

Maybe forty-six minutes might be long enough.

Except that the huge tree in the park was not strung with any lights.

Alex turned her attention to a much more manageable problem—the tree in front of her. She needed to put the star on, but the tree was too tall for her to reach the top from the floor. Ray was lost in the movie, and she decided not to disturb him. And after all, she was Alex Mack—the girl endowed with amazing powers, compliments of GC-161. She didn't need to stand on anything. She simply "thought" the star to the top, then telekinetically raised a string of lights into the air.

She froze, watching the light string hover over the top branches. This tree was only six feet tall. The tree in the park was ten times as high. She couldn't possibly string it with ten thousand lights. It was an impossible feat. . . .

Nothing is impossible. That's what Santa had told her.

Alex wasn't so convinced Santa was right. There was nothing she could do to help Annie with her scholarship exam or her dad with his acne medicine. She couldn't telekinetically whisk her mother home from the capital or force Ray to talk to his father. Stringing the park tree with ten thousand lights and keeping them lit for forty-six minutes seemed like an impossible job, too.

Alex shook off her momentary doubt and told herself she had nothing to lose by trying.

CHAPTER 12

Alex didn't have a minute to herself over the weekend. Ray had finally pitched in to help her finish decorating the tree Friday night. As they straggled in one by one, Annie and her parents had smiled in appreciation before retiring after their exhausting day. It wasn't quite the reaction Alex had hoped for, but it was a start.

Saturday Annie took over the bedroom for her studies and her mother set up shop in the living room and kitchen because she wanted to be home even though she had to work. Schedules and statistic reports covered the kitchen table, and campaign posters with different slogans occupied the couch and dining room chairs.

Mr. Mack had practically moved into the plant, coming home late to catch a couple hours of sleep before returning to the lab at dawn. Alex spent most of her weekend at the workshop. With Christmas only a few days away, the elves were working at a frantic pace to fill all of Santa's orders.

Alex didn't say a word to anyone about her plan to light the park tree for forty-six glorious minutes. For one thing, she didn't know if she could get the lights on the tree. If she succeeded, then she wanted it to be a surprise. The element of surprise would add to the townspeople's moment of Christmas wonder and joy.

The workshop was bustling with frenzied activity Sunday. Alex ran between Mr. Russo's temporary workshop office and the repair rooms with lists of finished toys and helped Robyn arrange everything on the shelves in alphabetical order by each child's last name. Being busy kept her from thinking about the monstrous job she had to do in the park that night. It was the night before Christmas Eve, and there were many secret preparations to be made before the tree was actually lit up the next night.

"What's the matter, Mr. Russo?" Alex asked

as she handed him another list. He was frowning at his computer screen.

"The *don't have* list just keeps getting longer." Mr. Russo sighed and pushed the print button.

Alex watched the ever-growing list printout. The under-six set had simple Santa orders, such as dolls and trucks, which were easy to fill. The older children were asking for toys that were new on the market and the current rage. A few people in town had bought and donated some of the specific items, but not nearly enough.

Mr. Russo glanced at Alex. "Don't worry, Alex. I'll think of something."

"I hope so. I'm out of ideas at the moment," Alex said.

Back in the shop, Mr. Thompson called her over to his workbench. He needed parts and asked her to see if Ray could scrounge them from the piles of unusable toys in another room. He unclipped his list from one of several clothes-pins attached to an unpainted board hanging on the wall.

Alex took the list, but her gaze was fastened on the board. "Does that belong to Mr. Russo?"

"No. Mr. Engles and I made several of those to help everyone keep organized. Why?"

"My sister could use something like that. We share a room and there's not a lot of space."

"Alex!" Louis hollered from across the room. "Mr. Russo wants to see you."

"See you later, Mr. Thompson." Waving, Alex ran off. She gave Louis the list to take to Raymond, then ducked back into Mr. Russo's office. Nicole was with him, straightening a stack of papers as they came off the printer.

"Nicole has an idea, Alex," Mr. Russo said.

"Since you've already visited all the stores in town and at the mall, you're the perfect person for this job," Nicole said.

"What job?"

Nicole handed her the pile of papers. "These are copies of the list of toys we're missing. Fifty-three to be exact. If every store in town just contributed one of these items, we could cover it."

Mr. Russo stood up. "Every item has a number. They can call and tell us which one they want to donate so we don't have any duplications."

Delivering the lists and explaining the problem took Alex the rest of the day. It was a discouraging job. Thanks to Mr. Hardwick's article in the newspaper and the town grapevine, everyone knew about the workshop and the elves. But that didn't alter the reality of everyone's dismal financial situations. Wanting to help and being able to help were two different things.

It was after dark when Alex got home and checked in with the workshop office.

Nicole answered the phone. "It wasn't a total waste of time, Alex. Eight people called and promised to bring us new toys."

"So we're still forty-five toys short."

"Yeah, but we have eight more than we did this morning, and there's still tomorrow," Nicole said.

Alex couldn't argue with that. Something was better than nothing. And it was nice to know that Nicole's fighting spirit was operating at full capacity again. Turning off the living room lights, Alex went upstairs to lie down. She was tired after running around town all day, and she had a long night ahead of her.

Annie was asleep at her desk, her cheek flat against a textbook. She started awake even though Alex was careful not to make any noise.

"Maybe you should just go to bed early, Annie. You won't do well on that exam Friday if you wear yourself out."

"I tried that." Bleary-eyed and yawning,

Annie straightened in her chair. "But as soon as I lie down I start thinking about what my life will be like if I don't go to college, and then I start worrying about everything and I can't sleep. So I might as well study."

Alex kicked off her shoes and flopped onto her bed. "There's no way you're *not* going to college. You're a genius, remember. If you don't get this scholarship, you'll get another one. Besides, Dad is working on something that will pull the plant and its employees out of this mess."

"I know. He showed me the formula for Ac-Not."

"Then why are you driving yourself like this?" Alex was mystified.

"Because . . ." Annie sighed and pushed her hair behind her ear. "Because I just can't stand the thought of having Christmas without Mom. If I wasn't exhausted and buried in books, I wouldn't be able to stop thinking about it. I think Dad's kinda doing the same thing. He's focused on the situation at the plant so he won't dwell on it, either."

Alex sat up. "Mom's gonna be here."

"No way, Alex. Not unless she sprouts wings and flies. *You* can't even do that."

"She'll be here," Alex said stubbornly. Like Annie and her dad, Alex had devoted herself to the toy drive so she wouldn't be depressed thinking about her mother's absence on Christmas. Now, faced with Annie's certainty that nothing could change the situation, she realized that she had to believe—really believe—that somehow her mother would find a way home for Christmas. They all had to believe . . . or it wouldn't happen.

"How can you be so sure, Alex?"

"I asked Santa Claus."

Annie didn't laugh. She just stared at Alex as though she'd lost her mind.

CHAPTER 13

At ten P.M. Alex waited on the sidewalk in front of Ray's house, pacing back and forth to keep warm. It was so cold she could see her breath.

Her mother was inside packing to catch an early morning flight with Mr. Houston and his campaign manager. Annie had fallen into a restless sleep, and her father was wandering around the house trying *not* to look upset. No one had questioned Alex's excuse for going out so late. They knew the elves were working round-the-clock to complete the needed toys.

Ray slipped out the door and into his jacket as he jogged down the walk. "What's up, Alex?"

Alex hadn't told him anything yet. She had

just called to say she needed his help. "You told me we couldn't fix a whole town, but we're gonna try," Alex said.

Ray blinked, then shrugged. "Why not? A week ago I didn't think the toy drive had a chance in a million of getting enough stuff for all those kids. I was sure wrong about that."

"So you'll help?"

"Just call me super-elf. What's the plan?"

Alex outlined her idea as they made their way through the deserted streets to the park.

"Now I wish I hadn't bought those Rocket Ranger action figures for the toy drive. I'm broke." Ray pulled his empty jacket pockets inside out. "I don't have enough left to buy even an extra minute of electricity for the tree."

"I didn't know you donated those action figures, Ray."

"Nobody does. I told Mr. Russo the guy wanted to remain anonymous." Ray looked at her pointedly. "And he does."

"Your secret's safe with me."

After ducking through the split-rail fence enclosing the park, Alex moved swiftly across the open grassland toward the grove of trees in the center. Ray followed silently behind her. There weren't any security guards on duty at night during the winter, but the police patrolled the area. Even though she intended to pay, Alex didn't want to get herself or Ray into trouble for using city electricity without permission. And the unexpected lighting of the tree wouldn't be quite so effective if the responsible parties were identified. A certain aura of mystery had to surround the event to give it that magical quality people associated with the holidays.

They reached the storage shed where the lights were kept without incident. It was situated a short distance from the giant fir. However, when Alex tried the door, she found it locked.

"Guess I'll have to morph," Alex whispered.

"Guess so," Ray agreed. "It's either that or break the lock."

"I'll morph." Concentrating, Alex dissolved into a puddle of silvery ooze. The warm tingles she felt during the transformation process quickly gave way to chilled shivers. The temperature had dropped drastically again. She had recently discovered that she moved slower and could stay morphed longer in cold temperatures, but she didn't know what to expect if she stayed morphed too long when it was freezing.

Sliding sluggishly under a crack between the door and floor, Alex slowly materialized inside.

She spotted a light switch by the door and zapped it on, the electrical energy shooting from her fingers warming her cold hands. She spoke to Ray through the closed door. "I'm going to find the lights and pile them by the door before I open it."

"Why? I thought you wanted me to help."

"I can't open the door with the light on. Someone might see. Just keep a lookout."

"Right."

Large cartons, each of them containing several heavy-duty strings of outdoor lights, were stacked along the back wall. The city meter was on the side wall. A bare spot beside it indicated where Danielle Atron's second meter should have been. Several coiled, thick electrical cords hung on hooks on the wall. There were two electrical outlets on the opposite wall. She made a mental note to check for outside plug-in sources. Then she tried levitating the boxes, but they were too heavy. Pushing with a combination of telekinesis and muscle, Alex finally got the boxes moved across the shed. Then she turned off the light, unlocked the door, and opened it.

"How'd you move these by yourself?" Ray grunted as he dragged one of the cartons outside. "Never mind. I know. . . ."

"It wasn't easy, either." Alex pushed as Ray pulled the other boxes out the door. When they were all outside, Alex checked the outer walls of the shed and found an outlet almost immediately. However, it took ten minutes to untangle the first strand of lights.

"My grandfather would have a fit," Alex said as she undid the last knot. "He's one of those people who very carefully loops the wire so that all the bulbs are at one end, then binds it with a twist tie so it stays neat. He saves tinsel icicles just as carefully. I think he's got tinsel icicles that are older than me."

"So that's where Annie gets her organizational streak." Ray picked up the looped strand and they started toward the tree.

Alex giggled. "I guess, but Annie never rolls up the after-dinner garbage in a brown paper bag and ties it with string before she throws it away."

"Gift-wrapped garbage? Why would anyone do that?"

"He says it satisfies his sense of order in the universe." Alex grinned, then noticed Ray's troubled expression. "What's wrong?"

"These really are heavy, Alex." Ray's knees buckled slightly. He stumbled the last few feet and dropped the lights at the foot of the tree. "I don't know how you're gonna get them up to the top of that."

Alex followed Ray's gaze upward through the expanse of branches. She couldn't even see the top through the dense, green-needled boughs. Taking a deep breath, she looked down and focused on the lights. She managed to raise the whole string off the ground, but she couldn't hold it. The loops fell, but none of the bulbs broke.

"You can't do this, Alex. Even if you could lift them, it'll take all night to string the whole tree."

"I don't care how long it takes." Alex wasn't ready to give up. Just because it was hard, didn't mean it couldn't be done. Concentrating again, she raised just the end of the string and "thought" it upward through the lower branches. When the dangling strand began to get too heavy to hold, she draped the hovering, loose end over a branch. Then she telekinetically grabbed the center of the string, "thought" it upward, and draped the second half of the string over another branch.

Ray nodded as he got the picture. "It's kind of like a relay system. Half-a-strand at a time using the tree to hold the extra weight. It just might work."

"It's gotta work."

"It'll still take all night."

Alex shrugged. "Then it takes all night. Now give me a boost up."

"Up?" Ray's eyes narrowed. "Up where?"

"Into the tree. I can't reach the top from down here."

"No way," Ray said sternly. "It's too high, Alex. You might fall."

"I don't have to go very high. I just need to be able to see the top." Alex pointed to a large, sturdy branch fifteen feet up the trunk. "That one's about right."

"I don't know . . ."

"Look," Alex said desperately, "if I feel myself starting to slip, I'll morph and slide down."

Giving in, Ray gave her a leg up into the branch just above her head. Settling into the angle where the large branch met the trunk, Alex began the slow and tedious process of raising the lights half a strand by half a strand to the top. Once convinced that Alex was secure in her perch, Ray moved far enough away to call out directions as she twined the strings through the upper branches.

Hour after hour, branch after branch, Alex telekinetically positioned the lights. An occasional car drove down the street bordering the park, but it was too dark and the two kids were too far away to be seen. The brutal cold was also an unexpected ally. Nobody had ventured out for a midnight stroll on the park paths.

Excitement and adrenaline kept Alex's weariness from hampering her progress as the night wore on. She took telekinetic breaks to plug the strings together by hand in an unbroken series. Ray gave her constant encouragement, and even the tree seemed protective. The one time she did feel herself slip slightly, her hand instinctively reached out and found a stabilizing branch. It was after three A.M. before she climbed down to finish the job from the ground. An hour later she and Ray put the empty cartons back in the shed.

"What are you doing with that?" Ray asked when Alex came out with a heavy-duty extension cord slung over her shoulder.

"I really don't want to have to morph into the shed again tomorrow. Stash this in the shrubs over there, and then I won't have to." Alex pointed to a clump of low evergreen bushes. The cord was black and wouldn't be visible unless someone was looking for it.

"What are you going to do?" Ray asked, taking the cord from her.

"I have to lock the door." Alex closed herself inside the shed, locked the door, then morphed to get out again. Ray was walking back from the bushes, staring over his shoulder at the tree with a thoughtful frown.

"Now what's the matter?" Alex asked.

"What if someone notices the lights on the tree tomorrow?"

"I don't think we have to worry about that. Everyone's bummed out because they think the tree *isn't* going to have lights. So they're staying away from the park."

Ray pulled Alex back against the wall of the shed as headlights appeared on the street along the park. The car passed without slowing. They waited a minute to be sure it was gone, then raced across the park to the fence.

Ray leaped over the top rail to the far side, then paused to look back at the dark silhouette of the tree. A slow smile spread across his tired face.

"What?" Alex asked.

Ray shrugged. "I was just imagining the expressions on everyone's faces when it suddenly lights up. It gives me goose bumps just thinking about it."

"Me, too."

Alex gazed at the tree and crossed her fingers.

CHAPTER 14

Alex arrived home just before her parents' alarm went off, two hours earlier than usual. She told her family she'd woken early to say good-bye to her mother so they wouldn't ask where she'd been till four A.M. Mr. Mack was showered and dressed within minutes so he could load the car to take his wife to the airport. Even Annie came downstairs. No one talked much. Their mutual sadness was understood, making words unnecessary.

After bidding her mother good-bye, Alex collapsed on the couch, but she couldn't fall asleep right away. Until the minute her father had driven out of the driveway, she had honestly believed something wondrous would happen to prevent her mother from getting on the plane. Now all hope was gone.

She slept most of the day, rising just long enough to call Nicole and explain that she wouldn't be able to get to the workshop. She didn't say why, but Nicole assured her that everything was under control. Except for the forty-five gifts on the *don't have* list, almost everything else was done and tagged. Most of the elf squad was taking a break to rest up for the Santa festivities starting at nine-thirty the next morning. Mr. Thompson, the Porter sisters, and a few others were hanging in to help Mr. Russo with the last-minute details. Nicole suspected they wanted to savor every minute before the workshop closed and they had to return to the routine of their normal lives.

Annie woke Alex up at four in the afternoon. Mumbling her thanks, Alex stumbled upstairs and into the shower. Twenty minutes later, feeling refreshed and awake, Alex collected the poinsettia bottles from under her bed. To keep the flowers from getting squashed, they were wrapped and packed in boxes she had found in the garage. Running ahead of schedule now, she even had time to finish listing the songs on her dad's tape before she and Ray left for the park. Christmas Eve was upon her and somehow she had managed to get everything done.

Alex was halfway across the living room before she noticed Annie had fallen asleep on the couch with the TV remote clutched in her hand. The TV was off. Moving quietly, Alex arranged the bottles under the tree by the few presents her parents had left. She still wished she had been able to get something special for Annie, but she also knew that Annie would approve of using her money for the town tree—if she knew, which she wouldn't.

Annie sat up suddenly. "How long have I been asleep?"

"Not long enough." Alex glanced at the boom box on the floor by the tree. Annie really needed some peace and quiet. Reaching down, Alex pulled the boom box plug. The digital-count list was still underneath it. She put it in her pocket. "Go back to sleep."

"Fifteen minutes," Annie muttered as she leaned back. "Wake me . . . up in fifteen . . . minutes. . . ." She was asleep again before her head hit the throw pillows.

"Right." Shaking her head, Alex grabbed her coat from the hall and checked her pocket to make sure the ten dollar bill was still there. Taking the boom box with her, she ducked into the garage. She hastily made a donation sign to collect funds for the lighting of the tree. Then she put it in a plastic bucket and went to Ray's.

"It's not five-thirty, yet, is it?" Ray rubbed sleep from his eyes as he opened the door.

"No, but I wanted some company." Alex glanced up at the overcast sky. The air was calm, but getting colder. She shivered. "Can I come in?"

"Sure." Ray followed her into the living room and watched as she plugged in the boom box. "What are you doing?" he asked.

"I've got to listen to the rest of this tape to double-check my play list. You've got headphones I can borrow, don't you? That way you won't have to listen."

"Don't worry about it. I've got to wash my face and stuff anyway."

While Ray went to get ready, Alex settled down with her list. Ray had rewound the tape too far, but the upbeat songs made her feel like her daring plan might *really* work. As "It's Beginning to Look Like Christmas" began to play, Alex noted the count.

Ray called down from upstairs. "Is my Raiders cap in the kitchen?"

"I'll check." Alex found the cap on the table and dashed back into the living room just as Raymond came bounding downstairs. . . .

And his father walked in the front door.

Alex froze. She remembered what Ray had said about his dad—he couldn't stand listening to Christmas music.

"Dad! What are you doing home now?" Ray asked.

"They let everyone off early." Mr. Alvarado moved toward the kitchen as he shrugged out of his jacket. He stopped suddenly and snapped his head toward the music coming from the boom box. "Please turn that off," he said softly. Then he continued down the hall without looking back.

Alex sprang to hit the off button just as Ray grabbed his coat off a chair and picked hers up from the living room floor. "Let's go!"

Confused by the conflicting demands, Alex hesitated. "The music—"

The song ended abruptly, filling the house with silence.

"Tape's over. Let's go!"

"It can't be over. There's more—" Alex didn't

have a chance to finish her sentence. Ray took her hand and yanked her outside.

Alex looked at the closed door as she paused on the stoop to put on her coat. She was sure there were more songs on the tape. Unless they had gotten erased somehow . . .

"I'm sorry, Alex," Ray said, "but I just had to get out of there. I don't want anything to spoil the fun, you know?"

"Yeah, but I'm the one who's sorry, Ray. I didn't mean to upset him like that."

"You didn't do anything, Alex. It's just bad timing. If I had known the plant was going to let out early, I would have given you the head-phones." Inhaling to calm himself, Ray forced a smile. "And don't worry about your boom box. I'll get it for you later."

"Okay, thanks."

"Now let's go light up a tree. So what if my dad's grumpy. At least we might be able to fix the rest of this town."

"I sure hope so."

As they started down the sidewalk, Mr. Mack pulled into the driveway. He waved and smiled as he stepped out. "Hey, kids!"

"Hi, Dad!" Alex ran over. "You got off early, huh?"

"Well, the lab results of the acne medication are in and they're as promising as I hoped. The report's on Ms. Atron's desk, and there's nothing more I can do. Besides, it's Christmas Eve and I belong here with my girls. Especially since your mom—" Mr. Mack's smile tightened.

"Uh—I gotta go," Alex said, shifting from foot to foot.

"Go?" Mr. Mack looked stricken. "Where?"

"Elf business!" Ray grinned. "Important elf business."

"Oh." Mr. Mack nodded solemnly. "Well, that's okay, then. From what I hear, there's going to be a lot of happy kids tomorrow morning because of you guys."

"Thanks to you, Dad."

"Me? I didn't do anything."

"Yes, you did." Alex fumbled for the right words. "You helped me a lot."

"How?" Mr. Mack frowned, totally baffled. "I've hardly seen you in the past two weeks."

"Right. Because you've been working hard and not giving up against impossible odds. I've just been following your example."

"Oh, I see." Mr. Mack nodded, but he still looked perplexed.

Ray and Alex started off. "This would be a

nice night to take a walk by the park," Alex said, trying to act as casual as possible.

"There's a ten percent chance of snow!" Mr. Mack hollered after them.

"Really? That's perfect!" Waving, Alex and Ray dashed off.

Mr. Alvarado stood in front of the stove, waiting for the water to boil and trying not to lose his temper. Ray knew how difficult the holidays were for him. He shouldn't have invited Alex over, especially to play Christmas music. They reminded him too painfully of the past.

He jumped, hearing voices in the front room.

Scowling, Mr. Alvarado listened. Nothing. He spooned instant coffee into his mug and heard the voices start up again.

Was someone in the house? Mr. Alvarado stormed down the hall.

"It's okay, Alex."

Ray's voice? But Ray just left, Mr. Alvarado thought.

He stopped and looked at the boom box on the floor of the living room. Ray's conversation with Alex had inadvertently been recorded. Stunned, Mr. Alvarado realized they were discussing him.

"It's not your fault my dad is being such a jerk—again," Ray said.

As his son spoke to him from the speakers, Mr. Alvarado's eyes filled with tears.

The sun was just sinking below the horizon when Alex and Ray reached the fence surrounding the park. Alex looked out over the grassy field and felt a rush of sadness. If this was a normal year, the field would be dotted with bonfires and booths serving hot chocolate, cookies, and apple-cinnamon doughnuts. Families would be standing in groups, laughing, talking, and singing carols while they waited for the mayor to throw the switch. A huge cheer would ring out as the tree lit up the dark sky. But this Christmas Eve was truly a silent night. The park was dark and deserted.

Almost.

"What's a park attendant doing here?" Ray whispered from the clump of evergreen shrubs where the extension cord was hidden.

"Maybe he's guarding the place against people like us." Alex stared at the man sitting in a chair by the storage shed. She couldn't believe they had come so far only to reach such a major roadblock.

CHAPTER 15

We've come so far. There's got to be a way to light the tree, Alex told herself.

She studied the guard in the waning light. A flashlight rested in his lap, and a cellular phone dangled from his belt. He looked bored, but he was awake. Even in the dark, Alex and Ray couldn't connect the extension cord to the tree lights, uncoil it, and plug it into the shed outlet without the man noticing.

"Maybe he'll leave to go do his rounds or something," Ray suggested. "Like the security guys at the plant."

"Maybe. And maybe he won't."

"You'll have to zap them on," Ray stated matter-of-factly.

"I can't zap ten thousand lights, Ray!"

"How many can you zap?"

Alex shrugged. "I don't know. Ten? A hundred?"

"That's not very many."

"No . . . but maybe it'll be enough to distract the guard."

"Then what?" Ray's worried frown changed into a grin that got wider and wider as Alex explained her idea. First she had to get the guard's attention—without his actually knowing what was happening.

They waited until the last, lingering rays of the setting sun faded. Except to stretch, yawn, and check his watch, the guard hadn't moved.

"Be careful," Ray said as Alex prepared to carry out the first part of the plan.

Nodding, Alex took a deep breath and morphed. As her solid cells changed to liquid, she experienced a rush of anxiety mingled with excitement. If the guard suddenly decided to check the area with his flashlight before she reached the tree, she had no place to hide.

Slithering out of the shrubs, Alex glided to the base of the towering tree. The cold seeped into her liquified cells, slowing her movements. Gripping the rough bark, Alex began to crawl upward. She knew she looked like a giant, silvery slug. And although she was on the far side of the tree, hidden from the guard's sight by the massive trunk, she felt more exposed and vulnerable than she had on the ground. Minutes passed as she pulled herself up into the safety of the large branch that had been her roost the night before. Seconds after puddling in the angle where the branch met the trunk, she materialized.

Heaving a sigh of relief, Alex took a moment to catch her breath. Then she looked down toward the shrubs. She couldn't see anything but vague outlines in the dark. Reaching out with her thoughts, she "felt" along the ground until she "touched" the end of the extension cord Ray had poked through the evergreen branches. *Step two*, she thought as she telekinetically snagged the cord. The dry grass rustled slightly as she mentally dragged the black cable over the ground toward the tree.

When the end of the cord reached the tree, Alex paused to glance at the guard. It was difficult to tell for sure, but it looked like his chin was resting on his chest, as though he had dozed off. Grabbing the end of the cord again, Alex "thought" it upward into her hand. After finding the plug on the end of the last light string, she connected it to the extension cord. Then she waited.

Ray couldn't see her very well in the dark. She had had to estimate how long it would take to complete the cord connection. He wouldn't make his move until the fifteen minutes had passed.

Finally, Alex saw his shadowy form creep out of the shrubs. He was holding the plug-in end of the extension cord in one hand and had the donation bucket tucked under his other arm. Trailing the cord behind him, he darted across a ten-foot open space to the semicircle of smaller evergreen trees growing behind the giant fir. She gave him another three minutes to get into position behind the last tree in the row. Another twenty-foot open space was all that separated him from the outlet on the shed.

Well, here goes nothing. . . . Raising her arm, Alex shot a zapper high into the tree. Lights flashed in the upper branches and went off. She zapped again. Another set of lights flashed and glowed before darkening.

"What!" The guard was on his feet in an instant, but he didn't move away from the shed. He just stood there, staring at the tree as lights flashed here and there among the branches.

"Did you see that?" Another man with a dog on a leash darted across the grass to join the guard.

"I sure did," the guard said. "Thought I was going crazy there for a minute."

"I come to watch the tree lighting every year," the other man said. "Didn't expect to see it tonight, though. I was just out walking Bootsie."

Come on, you guys, Alex thought as she zapped. *Move!* Ray couldn't plug in the cord while the two men were standing there.

The guard whipped out his cellular phone. "Hey, Barney!" he shouted into the mouthpiece. "You're not gonna believe this, but the town tree's lighting itself!" He paused. "Impossible my eye. I'm watching it with another guy!"

Alex zapped, spacing the bolts of electricity so she wouldn't tire too quickly. It was lucky for her the guard wasn't too anxious to investigate. She'd have to morph and hide fast if he came too close with his flashlight.

"Oh, no!" Annie's voice rang out through the night.

Uh-oh. Alex looked out to see her father and sister strolling across the field.

"Will you look at that!" Mr. Mack exclaimed as he and Annie broke into a jog.

Cars passing by squealed to a stop. People piled out of them and raced toward the tree. Porch lights in the houses across the street from the park went on as parents and children ran outside. Alex continued to zap intermittently.

From her high perch Alex could see the glow of headlights turning on all over Paradise Valley. She struggled to stay calm as more and more people streamed into the park. She hadn't thought about how to get out of the tree with a crowd watching.

Finally, the guard and the man with the dog walked over to join the excited people converging on the tree. Timing was critical now. Alex had to move quickly to avoid being seen when Ray plugged in the lights.

She saw Ray dash out of hiding toward the shed.

Below her men, women, and children formed a circle around the tree, cutting off her escape route down the trunk. Eyes wide with wonder and anticipation, they stared up into the dark branches.

Ray reached the shed and fell to his knees.

Alex morphed.

And the crowd gasped as the Paradise Valley Christmas tree blazed with the brilliance of ten thousand lights.

CHAPTER 16

In her morphed state, Alex flattened herself on a branch on the back side of the trunk and slowly oozed outward. The blinding glow of so many lights acted as a shield. As she inched along, she caught snatches of conversation below.

"Ms. Atron must have changed her mind at the last minute," one man suggested.

"Maybe things at the plant aren't as bad as she thought," a woman offered hopefully.

"But why did only some of the lights flash before they all came on?" a little boy asked.

"A short circuit maybe." His mother shrugged.

"I don't care how," someone else said. "I'm

just glad they're on. Now it really seems like Christmas.''

"It sure warms my heart," said a smiling young woman.

Alex saw the guard frown and scratch his head as he turned and walked away.

A lone voice began to sing "Oh, Christmas Tree." Soon everyone was singing along.

The branch began to bend under her weight as Alex slid farther out. Then the end of the branch caught on the upper branches of an evergreen in the semicircle of shorter trees behind the Christmas tree. In danger of materializing any second, Alex slithered faster. She oozed into the top of the short tree, and the towering fir's lighted branch, now relieved of her weight, snapped up. With no time to spare, Alex glided to the ground down the trunk of the smaller tree.

She materialized almost immediately and found herself staring into Annie's scowling face. Ray, who'd been scouting the row of trees looking for her, hurried over.

"What do you think you're doing, Alex Mack?" Annie demanded.

First Alex glanced around the area to make sure her father wasn't nearby. Then she met her sister's stern gaze without wavering and said,

"Lighting the town tree so everyone will feel better."

"Well—" Annie's scowl slowly dissolved and was replaced by a beaming smile. "I've got to hand it to you this time, Alex," she said. "Your plan really worked! I do feel better. And so do a lot of other people."

"Yeah!" Laughing, Alex dashed out from behind the trees. Families and groups of friends were still arriving. The crowd around the tree was singing "Deck the Halls" while others stood back to laugh and talk. Children were dispatched to gather fallen tree branches for a bonfire the fire chief was building in a pit, as was the tradition.

Mr. Larkin, the owner of the toy store, was surrounded by people Alex recognized—several managers and store owners she had given the *don't have* list to yesterday. The toy store owner was nodding, collecting money, and writing furiously in a memo book as people pledged donations. If this was any indication, Alex was sure the workshop would have all forty-five of the missing toys by tomorrow morning.

"The only thing that's missing is the hot chocolate and doughnuts," Ray said.

"And Santa Claus," Alex added.

"He's here." Annie pointed toward the shed. "I saw him over there a few minutes ago."

"I gotta talk to him," Alex said excitedly. "Be right back."

"Right." Annie rolled her eyes. "I'll look for Dad."

"I smell doughnuts." Sniffing, Ray wandered away.

As Alex skirted the crowd, she saw four police cars parked by the curb. Her heart fluttered, but the officers weren't there to investigate the unofficial lighting of the tree. They were walking across the field carrying boxes and boxes of doughnuts.

And following behind them was Mr. Alvarado.

Alex held her breath as Ray spotted his dad and stopped dead in his tracks. Time seemed to stand still as father and son stared at each other. Then Mr. Alvarado opened his arms. Ray didn't hesitate to accept his dad's bear hug embrace.

Then one of the policemen split off from the others to join the guard by the shed. Alex spotted Santa and continued walking toward him, but she kept her eyes and ears on the two men by the shed.

The guard turned on his flashlight and directed the beam at the outlet. "Someone plugged it into city power."

The policeman looked uncomfortable. "See all these happy people? I can't arrest anyone for breaking into the shed and stealing power to light the tree! They'd run me out of town."

"Well, that may not be a problem." The guard picked up the plastic bucket and pulled out Alex's ten dollar bill. "Someone has paid for forty-six minutes already. Sign says it'll take nine hundred dollars to keep the tree lit all week."

"How long has it been on?" the officer asked.

The guard checked his watch. "Eighteen minutes."

The policeman dug into his jacket and dropped a five dollar bill into the bucket. "That's another twenty-three." Then he took the bucket and began to circulate through the crowd.

"Alex!" Mr. Mack called. "Over here!"

Alex hurried toward him, surprised to see he was talking with Santa. "Hi, Dad! How long have you known Santa Claus?"

"This is Mr. Wilcox, Alex. His son, Dan, works with me in the lab."

Alex grinned, thinking, *So that's how he knew my name!*

Santa winked. "From what my son tells me, Alex, your dad is the *real* Santa Claus this year. That Ac-Not stuff he came up with will keep everyone in town working."

"My dad's pretty cool, all right."

Mr. Mack shrugged self-consciously.

"Dad!" Annie waved from the crowd. "Can you come here a minute! They're taking up a collection to keep the tree going."

Mr. Mack shook hands with Mr. Wilcox, then turned to Alex. "Coming?"

"In a minute." As she watched her father leave, Alex saw the gray hearse from Russo's Funeral Home screech to a halt on the street. It was decorated with green garlands, red bows, and covered with twinkling Christmas lights. Mr. Russo, Nicole, Robyn, Mr. Thompson, the Porter sisters, and Ms. Clark got out. Alex giggled and said to Mr. Wilcox, "The elf squad just arrived in the elf mobile."

Santa laughed and waved as the workshop crew came toward them. "Wonderful. Now everyone's here who should be."

Not quite everyone, Alex thought, her high spirits dropping like a weight. Her mother wasn't there, but she wasn't going to ruin Mr. Wilcox's fun by reminding him. Except it was too late to cover herself, she realized as she looked back. He had already seen the disappointment written all over her face.

"What's going on?" Mr. Thompson asked, planting his hands on his hips as he stared at the tree. "Thought they weren't going to light it this year."

Santa's face remained solemn. "Seems Paradise Valley has a couple of Christmas elves working undercover." He looked at Alex pointedly.

He can't know I did it! Alex lowered her gaze, wondering. Mr. Wilcox was just an ordinary man who liked to play Santa Claus at Christmas. Still . . . there was something about him.

"What happened to Robyn and Nicole?" Alex asked, to change the subject.

"They're by the tree, dear," Mabel Porter said, pointing.

"Thanks." As Alex walked away, Mr. Wilcox called to her.

"Alex. Wait a minute. . . ."

"I'll see you all later, okay?" Alex kept going, but she heard Mr. Thompson question Mr. Wilcox.

"Why are you looking so glum, Santa? This is turning out to be the best Christmas ever."

"For a lot of people, it is. Not for Alex," Mr. Wilcox said sadly. "The only thing she wants for Christmas is to have her mother home to share it."

"And that's a problem?" Mr. Thompson asked.

"Yeah," Santa sighed wearily. "That's a problem."

Alex ran to join her friends. As bad as she felt because her mother was hundreds of miles away, she felt almost as bad for Mr. Wilcox. He so thoroughly enjoyed pretending to be Santa Claus, he had honestly believed he could make the impossible happen.

But Mr. Wilcox wasn't Santa Claus.

He didn't have a sleigh and eight flying reindeer that could magically bring her mother home, like in the movies.

Developing acne formulas and getting people to work together for a good cause and stringing lights on a tree were difficult tasks, but not impossible. Persistence combined with hard work had made those seemingly impossible goals possible. Alex looked up at the tree, then scanned the hundreds of smiling faces that had all been wearing frowns a short while ago.

And all it had taken was lights on a tree.

Then her gaze settled on Ray and his father. They were standing by the bonfire, eating doughnuts and swaying in time to a rowdy rendition of "Jingle Bell Rock."

Impossible. That's what Ray would have said only a couple of hours ago. But he would have been wrong. Mr. Alvarado was singing along at the top of his lungs. It occurred to Alex then that the perfect present for Ray—and his father—was a copy of the songs she had taped for her dad. The Alvarados needed music in their home.

A large snowflake settled on Alex's nose, surprising her. Then another. The crowd whistled and cheered as more and more white fluffy flakes drifted gently down from the sky.

. . . a ten-percent chance of snow . . . That's what her dad had told her. Those weren't good odds, but look what had happened.

Maybe Mr. Wilcox is right, Alex thought as a rush of emotion welled up inside her. *Maybe nothing is impossible.*

She closed her eyes, remembering how earnestly Mr. Wilcox had wanted her to believe in him. Believing might make all the difference. Besides, it wasn't fair to leave the kind old man thinking he had disappointed and disillusioned her, especially after all he had done to help the elf squad and the town's children.

She spun around to run back to him.

But Santa was gone.

CHAPTER 17

Alex woke up at six o'clock sharp the next morning.

Christmas.

She sat bolt upright in bed, instantly awake, and smiled. Ever since it had started snowing last night, she had not been able to shake the notion that her mother was on her way home. It didn't make any sense, but the absolute certainty wouldn't go away.

I'm probably just deluding myself, like Annie said, Alex thought as she swung her legs over the edge of the bed. She parted the curtain and gazed at a winter wonderland of lawns, trees, and houses covered with white Christmas snow.

Who said it never snowed in Paradise Valley? *And maybe Mr. Wilcox has a sleigh and eight tiny reindeer stashed in his garage.*

Muffling a giggle, she eased out of bed, gathered her clothes, and tiptoed out of the room. Annie and her father both wanted to sleep in. They had come home last night to find a message from her mother on the answering machine saying she wouldn't be getting back to her hotel until late. She had promised to call on Christmas.

Alex took a shower, then dressed and rushed downstairs. Her eyes landed on her boom box, sitting by the front door. She'd found it there when she'd returned from the park the night before. Ray must have dropped it off, knowing she'd need her father's Christmas tape.

Still mystified by the blank space she had heard yesterday, Alex picked up the boom box to take it into the kitchen to check. A paper sticking to the bottom fell off. It said: "Thanks, Alex. Mr. A."

She didn't have a clue why Ray's father was grateful to her. She was even more puzzled when she realized the last ten minutes of the tape had been completely erased. However, she knew what songs were missing. If she hurried and kept the volume on the stereo turned down, she could rerecord them in half an hour. Even though they had decided not to exchange gifts until her mother got home, Alex wouldn't be able to fix the tape after her father woke up. Once the tape was completed, she could record another one, with the volume off, for the Alvarados.

After a quick breakfast of cranberry juice and buttered toast, Alex turned on the Christmas tree lights and got to work.

The tape was finished at eight. It was wrapped and under the tree by eight-fifteen. At eight-twenty the doorbell rang, just as Annie trudged down the stairs in her bathrobe and slippers. "Who's at the door this early on Christmas morning?" she mumbled.

"Maybe it's Santa Claus," Alex quipped as she started toward the door.

"You've got Santa Claus on the brain," Annie said as she turned into the kitchen.

"Is someone ringing the doorbell?" Mr. Mack called from the upstairs hall.

"I'll get it, Dad." Alex threw open the door and squealed with delighted surprise. Mr. Wilcox, Mr. Thompson, Mrs. Grable, and the Porter sisters were standing in the front yard. Mr. Wilcox was wearing his Santa suit, and everyone else was bundled in coats, scarves, and knit hats. The elf mobile was parked in the driveway.

"What are you guys doing here?" Alex asked. "Shouldn't you be at the workshop getting ready for the big giveaway?"

"That's not for another hour," Irene Porter said. "And it can't start without us because we've got Santa Claus."

"Indeed," Mabel Porter agreed with an emphatic nod.

"Ho-ho-ho!" Mr. Wilcox grinned mischievously.

Alex smiled back, not sure why Mr. Wilcox was so amused, and asked the group, "Do you want to come in out of the cold?"

"And miss all this Christmas snow?" Santa Wilcox laughed.

"This is for you." Mr. Thompson handed Alex a huge bag. "Better stash it quick, 'cause it's not wrapped."

"What is it?" Alex peeked inside to find the clothespin clipboard that had been hanging on the workshop wall. Except now it was sanded and painted a country blue color with rose-colored heart decals. She had her special gift for Annie. "Thank you so much, Mr. Thompson!"

"What's going on?" Annie said.

Quickly stuffing the bag behind the bushes as

Annie came up behind her, Alex said, "It's just a few elves stopping by to say hi."

"Good morning," Mr. Mack said. Dressed, but with his hair still uncombed, he handed Alex her coat. Alex put it on and moved outside. Her father and Annie huddled in the doorway.

"What a great day for Christmas!" Ray grinned as he and his father walked up. Mr. Alvarado was carrying his toolbox. He winked at Ray and hid it behind his back.

"It's gonna be one to remember, that's for sure," Mr. Thompson said.

"Did you know they collected almost a thousand dollars to pay the electric bill for the town tree?" Irene Porter asked Alex.

"Enough to keep the tree lit every night through New Year's," Mabel added.

"Really? That's great news!" Alex said.

"And we've got some other good tidings we wanted to share with you, Alex," Mrs. Grable said.

"The elf squad workshop is going into operation year-round," Mabel Porter announced, bouncing with excitement.

"You're not closing down after today?" Mr. Mack asked.

"No, sir," Mr. Thompson said. "Mrs. Grable here, being the city financial officer and all, found out the town had money set aside for a senior citizens recreational facility that nobody's gotten around to building. So the town's going to rent that big garage from Mr. Russo."

"And we're going to keep right on collecting and fixing broken toys all year, so we'll be ready for next Christmas." Irene Porter sighed wistfully.

"And Robyn's father will use the rent money to fix the roof on the funeral home." Santa's eyes twinkled with glee. He grunted as Mr. Thompson looked down the block and nudged him in the side.

Everyone stared as a huge, eighteen-wheel, tractor-trailer rig rolled down the street and stopped in front of the house. The logo painted on the side read: NORTH POLE FROZEN FOOD TRANSPORT.

"Merry Christmas, Alex!" Mr. Wilcox bellowed, then laughed merrily.

"You got her a truckload of frozen food?" Ray looked at his dad. They both shrugged.

Alex started to tremble, unable to believe her eyes as the passenger door of the cab opened and her mother stepped out. Mrs. Mack was wearing one of her best black dinner dresses, black stockings, a pearl necklace, a camouflage army jacket, a fur-lined hat with earflaps, and lace-up hunting boots that were several sizes too big. She looked ridiculous—and she was the most beautiful sight Alex had ever seen. "Mom . . ." Alex cried out.

"I'm home!" Laughing, Mrs. Mack waved as she waded through the snow.

Annie stared at her mother in openmouthed astonishment.

Mr. Mack ran down the porch steps and threw his arms around her. "I can't believe it. Alex was so sure you'd be here—"

Mr. Wilcox looked at Alex with gentle, questioning eyes.

"I knew you could do it," Alex said.

"I had a lot of elf help."

"Darn right, he did. They don't call me 'Trucker' Thompson for nothing. I drove one of those rigs for forty years before I retired. I've still got a CB radio and a lot of old friends all over the country." Mr. Thompson nodded toward the man walking around the front of the cab. "Like Pothole there."

"I don't understand." Mr. Mack looked at Mrs. Mack narrowly. "Don't tell me you decided to hitchhike!"

"No." Mrs. Mack cuffed him playfully. "I got a phone call at the governor's benefit. A man named Dasher, who said he was reindeer number one, asked me to meet him in front of the hotel when I was finished, because Santa Claus had set up a trucker relay team to get me home."

"But he was still a stranger," Mr. Mack said sternly.

"Yes, dear," Mrs. Mack said patiently. "Dasher gave me Santa's phone number. I called Mr. Wilcox and he explained everything." She wiped a tear away and smiled. "Having me home was the only thing Alex wanted for Christmas."

"I'm so glad to see you!" Alex gave her mother a huge hug.

"I'm reindeer number four," the truck driver said. "Blitzen."

"Mr. Thompson said your name was Pothole." Ray frowned.

"It was—but it'll be Blitzen from now on. No way a guy can ever shake a story like this—or the handle that goes with it." The driver scowled at Mr. Thompson. "Thanks a lot, Trucker."

"Hey. It's not every road-jockey who gets to be a member of the Paradise Valley elf squad," Mr. Thompson countered. "Or who makes history that they'll still be talkin' about at truck stops twenty years from now."

"Speaking of elves, we do have to get Santa back to the workshop." Mabel patted the truck driver's arm. "You, too, Blitzen. Can't have Christmas without at least one of Santa's reindeer."

"Thanks." The driver beamed at Mr. Thompson. "I usually just work through the holidays, since I don't have any family."

"You do now." Mr. Thompson gripped the driver's shoulder and walked him back to his truck.

"You and your dad are coming along, aren't you, Ray?" Irene Porter asked.

Mr. Alvarado grinned and nodded. "We'll be along in a while. We've got some elf business of our own to take care of first."

"The railing and stuff," Ray whispered in Alex's ear.

Inside the phone rang. Annie went to answer it.

Mr. Alvarado turned to Mrs. Mack. "If that dinner invitation's still open, Ray and I would very much like to join you as usual."

"Of course, it's still open. Christmas dinner wouldn't be the same without you and Ray." Mrs. Mack's face glowed with pleasure as she started up the steps. "But we won't be eating until late this afternoon. We've got to go help the elf squad . . . as soon as I change."

Annie appeared in the doorway and held out the cordless phone. "It's for you, Dad."

Taking the phone, Mr. Mack paused on the porch. "I'm glad to hear you want to start making Ac-Not right away, Ms. Atron, but I can't come into the office to discuss it today. It's Christmas." He pushed the off button, squared his shoulders, and disappeared inside.

As the elves hurried toward the decorated hearse, Alex stopped Mr. Wilcox. "Thanks so much," she said. "I don't know what else to say. There are no words—"

"I'm the one who should be thanking you, Alex . . . for giving me a chance to find out what it feels like to be the real Santa Claus."

"As far as I'm concerned," Alex said honestly, "you *are* the real Santa Claus."

"That goes for me, too," Annie said from the doorway. "I'll never doubt you again, Santa."

Alex stared at her. Now she was positive that nothing, absolutely *nothing* was impossible.

"Merry Christmas!" Alex shouted and hugged her sister.

About the Author

Diana G. Gallagher lives in Kansas with her husband, Marty Burke, two dogs, three cats, and a cranky parrot. When she's not writing, she likes to read and take long walks with the dogs.

A Hugo Award–winning illustrator, she is best known for her series *Woof: The House Dragon*. Her songs about humanity's future are sung throughout the world and have been recorded in cassette form: "Cosmic Concepts More Complete," "Star*Song," and "Fire Dream." Diana and Marty, an Irish folksinger, perform traditional and original music at science-fiction conventions.

Her first adult novel, *The Alien Dark*, appeared in 1990. She is also the author of a *Star Trek: Deep Space Nine*® novel for young readers, *Arcade*, and several other books in *The Secret World of Alex Mack* series, all available from Minstrel Books.

She is currently working on another *Star Trek* novel and a new *Alex Mack* story.

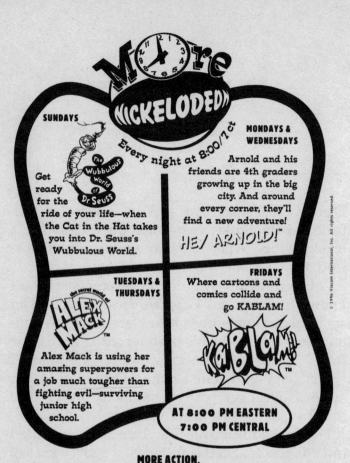

More NICKELODEON

Every night at 8:00/7 ct

SUNDAYS

The Wubbulous World of Dr. Seuss

Get ready for the ride of your life—when the Cat in the Hat takes you into Dr. Seuss's Wubbulous World.

MONDAYS & WEDNESDAYS

Arnold and his friends are 4th graders growing up in the big city. And around every corner, they'll find a new adventure!

HEY ARNOLD!™

TUESDAYS & THURSDAYS

the secret world of ALEX MACK™

Alex Mack is using her amazing superpowers for a job much tougher than fighting evil—surviving junior high school.

FRIDAYS

Where cartoons and comics collide and go KABLAM!

KABLAM!™

AT 8:00 PM EASTERN 7:00 PM CENTRAL

MORE ACTION.
MORE ADVENTURE. MORE SURPRISES.
MORE NICK! IT'S A HALF-HOUR MORE NICKELODEON EVERY WEEKNIGHT

ON THE ONLY NETWORK THAT GIVES YOU MORE OF WHAT YOU WANT, WHEN YOU WANT IT—NICKELODEON!

1276

A MINSTREL® BOOK
Published by Pocket Books

Simon & Schuster Mail Order Dept. BWB
200 Old Tappan Rd., Old Tappan, N.J. 07675

Please send me the books I have checked above. I am enclosing $_____(please add $0.75 to cover the postage and handling for each order. Please add appropriate sales tax). Send check or money order--no cash or C.O.D.'s please. Allow up to six weeks for delivery. For purchase over $10.00 you may use VISA: card number, expiration date and customer signature must be included.

Name _____

Address _____

City _____ State/Zip _____

VISA Card # _____ Exp.Date _____

Signature _____ 1053-10